A L

"I came here to talk, Jimmy Weak Dog. I have kept no secrets from you. Now you have no secrets from me. This is good. Now we can sit in the fire circle and talk as one man to another, you and me. Or would you dishonor your people and shoot me, instead? Pissing Horse gave me three days, Jimmy Weak Dog. Only one has passed. Would you shoot me now? If you do, Jimmy Weak Dog, you must shoot me as a coward shoots. You must shoot me in the back."

Longarm turned away and began walking back to the council fire.

There was a tiny spot of intense heat concentrated high on his back, just about midway between his shoulder blades. If any one of the Ute scouts fired at him, he figured, that should be about where the bullet would go.

Longarm focused his attention on keeping his gait loose and his manner easy as he strolled back toward the circle.

It was out of his hands now . . .

*   *   *

This title includes an exciting preview from *The Last Chance Kid* by Golden Spur Award–winning author Nelson Nye. *The Last Chance Kid* is available now from Jove Books.

Also in the LONGARM series
from Jove

TABOR EVANS

LONGARM

AND THE UTE NATION

JOVE BOOKS, NEW YORK

LONGARM AND THE UTE NATION

A Jove Book / published by arrangement with
the author

PRINTING HISTORY
Jove edition / February 1992

ISBN: 0-515-10790-5

Jove Books are published by The Berkley Publishing Group,
200 Madison Avenue, New York, New York 10016.
The name "JOVE" and the "J" logo
are trademarks belonging to Jove Publications, Inc.

10 9 8 7 6 5 4 3 2 1

LONGARM

AND THE
UTE NATION

Chapter 1

Longarm felt hot, dusty, tired, and just plain out of sorts. The sandwich he'd had on the Denver & Rio Grande had tasted like wood shavings, and some part of it must have been spoiled, because now his stomach was sour. He kept belching, and the flavor of secondhand pickle wasn't much to his liking.

"H'lo, Henry," he mumbled as he hung his Stetson on an arm of the coatrack in the United States marshal's office in Denver's Federal Building.

"Did you get your prisoner?" Henry asked.

Longarm nodded but didn't bother to speak. The assignment had been purely routine. Take a train ride south; collar the dumb S.O.B. of a postal employee who'd been pilfering from the till; take a train ride north again. The whole thing had taken less than a day.

"Check him into the stone hotel for the night?"

Longarm nodded again. The stone hotel was the county jail where federal prisoners were often housed.

"Talkative, aren't you," the marshal's chief clerk mused.

"It's that kinda day, Henry. Don't take it personal."

"Pretty country down there," Henry persisted, obviously looking for some sort of positive reaction from the tall deputy.

"Dammit, Henry, the only decent thing about Rye is its name. Now, leave me be, will you?" He took the signed-off arrest warrant and prisoner receipts out of a coat pocket and tossed them onto Henry's desk. "Look, why don't I just turn around and slip outa here. I'm not gonna be any good to anybody the rest of the day anyhow. I think I'll go over see if that pharmacist fella . . . What's his name? Cal Bowman's

1

brother; you know 'im . . . Anyway, dammit, I think I'll go by an' see if he has a stomach powder that's any good."

"You can't go yet, Longarm."

"Why the hell not?"

Henry inclined his head in the direction of the closed door that led into U.S. Marshal William Vail's office. "He said he wanted to see you when you got back."

"Dammit, Henry, I was lucky to get back here in daylight, much less during working hours. Just happened t' hit the connections. Why, by rights I shouldn't be reporting back here till tomorra morning anyhow, and you know it."

Henry gave him a searching look but didn't say anything. It was plain that if Longarm turned and walked out, Henry wouldn't peach on him. On the other hand, it was equally plain where Henry thought duty lay.

Actually, they both knew where duty lay. The trouble was that duty wasn't always convenient.

"Shit," Longarm muttered.

But he went to the door leading into Vail's office and not the one that would have taken him out into the hall.

"You wanted t' see me, boss?"

There were men, including men in high position, whom Custis Long would have been uncomfortable about calling boss. Billy Vail wasn't one of them. With Billy it seemed only right and proper for a deputy to be respectful. After all, mild and balding appearances aside, Billy Vail had been as good in the field as the best of them. And a damn sight better than most.

It wouldn't have occurred to Longarm to think about it, but he himself was in that "best" category that Billy could be compared to.

Unlike the marshal, though, Deputy Long looked the part of a lawman. Or peace officer, as he really preferred.

Longarm was several inches over six feet in height, with broad shoulders and a horseman's narrow waist and powerful legs. He had brown hair and a thick, sweeping brown mustache. His features were tanned and might have been chiseled out of walnut. Women found his rugged good looks appealing, which he failed to understand but found no reason to complain about.

He wore a brown tweed coat, brown corduroy trousers, and black stovepipe boots cut for comfort and walking rather than the stirrup. The butt of a Colt double-action .44 revolver rode in a crossdraw rig just to the left of his belt buckle, and there was a sturdy watch chain draped across the front of his vest. There was nothing in the appearance of the chain to suggest that instead of a fob Longarm carried a brass-framed derringer soldered to that end of the chain.

"Come in, Longarm. Sit down." Billy leaned back from the papers that covered most of the surface of his desk. A marshal's job was nearly all administrative, a fact that sometimes still seemed to rankle Vail. "Everything go all right in Rye?"

Longarm nodded. His cheeks puffed out a bit when he tried to contain another belch. Damn, it tasted foul. He could hardly accept that he'd eaten anything nasty enough to come back on him this hard.

"You don't look good, Longarm. Would you like to take a few days off?"

"I'm all right." It was one thing to bitch and moan when it was Henry he was talking to. It was something else entirely to show weakness in front of the boss. Billy might think he was trying to duck his fair share of things. And if Billy wouldn't actually think anything like that, well, Longarm would think that Billy *ought* to think it and feel guilty about saying it anyhow.

"You wouldn't lie to me, would you?" Billy asked.

"Only if I thought there was a reason to," Longarm said with a grin.

"Well, if you want out of this, just say so. It isn't like it's anything interesting. In fact, I've been debating whether I should send you at all."

Longarm raised an eyebrow. Indecision wasn't generally something that could be thought of in the same breath with Billy Vail.

"The deal is this, Longarm. You remember a lawyer named Able? A. B. Able?"

"Uh-huh." That was certainly true. He did remember A. B. Able. Not that he wanted to elaborate on the memories with his employer.

3

Lawyer Able had been involved in a case Longarm drew a little while back down in southwestern Colorado at a mountain mining camp called Snowshoe. The case was only supposed to require service of a writ of habeas corpus to secure the release of some Ute Indians who were A. B. Able's clients. In fact, it had become considerable more complicated than that, having to do with railroads and gold theft and old-fashioned greed. The poor Ute had simply been unlucky enough to see the thieves spiriting their loot away, and all the legal foofaraw was an attempt to keep them quiet. The silly thing of it was that the Ute hadn't given a fat crap about either the gold or the white men who were stealing it, and in fact, hadn't paid any attention to what they witnessed. If the thieves had left well enough alone, they might even have gotten away with their scheme. As it turned out, Longarm cooperated with the local lawmen and put the dummies behind bars.

Billy Vail, of course, knew all of that. It had all been detailed in the report Longarm filed after he returned to Denver.

What Longarm didn't think he'd ever bothered to write down or particularly mention was that Lawyer Able's first name wasn't Abner or Abraham or anything sensible like that. It was Agnes. Otherwise known as Aggie. And Aggie was one of the best-looking damned women Custis Long ever put an eye to. She was also, sadly, one of the sloppiest, poorest, most inept and unenjoyable lays he'd ever had in his life.

Another assignment that would take him within reach of Aggie Able was not his idea of fun and good times.

"Apparently, the Ute nation has retained Able again, Longarm, and once again he has requested that you be assigned to the case. His message cites the usual reasons, preexisting conditions of confidence placed in you by the Ute, knowledge of and acceptance by individual tribe members, that sort of thing."

"You don't sound very impressed, boss."

"I would be if I thought we had a case to get into, Longarm. But frankly, I'm not sure that we do."

"Oh?"

"Able has been hired to secure the release of a Ute warrior who is employed by the army as a scout. His name is Bird Talks to the Moon. More or less."

Longarm nodded. Close was often as good as it got when you were trying to translate some things, names in particular, from Indian tongues into English.

"So what's Bird's problem, Billy?"

"He's being held under guard on suspicion of murder."

"Suspicion only?"

"That's right—he hasn't been charged with anything. And if he is, it will be a military matter, anyway. The dead men were all military. A major who was supposed to assume command of a new agency detachment in eastern Utah and two men who were escorting the major to his new billet. One officer and two enlisted, all of them army."

"And Bird was enrolled as a scout?"

"That's right."

"Shit, Billy, we don't have jurisdiction. Not unless the army asks for our assistance."

"That was my reading on it, too, Longarm. Except I have one or two niggling little doubts that I can't quite get out of my mind."

"Oh?"

"One is that A. B. Able seems to know the law as well as anyone. He was quick enough to take advantage of precedent after that first habeas corpus ruling in Nebraska."

Longarm nodded. The Nebraska case had been an obscure one. And not necessarily popular. It advanced the silly notion that Indians might have rights just like human people did. Not everybody wanted to accept that outlandish theory.

"What little I heard about Able during that case, Longarm, makes me think the man might be sharp enough to have come up with some excuse for bringing the Justice Department in over the heads of the Department of the Army."

"I didn't know we were in the business of looking for ways to piss off army generals, boss."

"We, um, aren't. But if you'll recall, I did say there were several doubts nagging at me."

"Uh-huh."

"The other one is that this request came in just after you left here this morning. I spent half the day sending telegraph messages back and forth between here and Green River. The one in Wyoming, that is, not in Utah. That's where Able is and

5

where the army's relay telegrapher is supposed to be, too."

"Supposed to be?"

"I'm getting information only from Mr. Able, Longarm. The army has refused to respond to any of my requests for information. They acknowledged receipt of my first inquiry. Not a peep out of them since. The Western Union telegrapher here tells me he hasn't been able to raise the Green River army operator since shortly after my message was receipted. Apparently, they've closed their key there."

"That's funny."

"Damned funny," Billy agreed.

"Kinda does make a body wonder. But I'd still have t' say we got no jurisdiction."

"Not about that, Longarm. Not a bit of it," Billy said. He had one of those self-satisfied smiles on his face that said he was up to something.

"What d'you have in mind, boss?"

"Do you remember that last month we got a tip that Clete Bacon was in Brown's Hole, maybe heading toward Vernal?"

"No, not really."

"Trust me. We got a tip about that."

"If you say so," Longarm agreed. Hell, they were all the time getting tips. Most of which were worth everything they cost. Which was zero. If a guy wanted to pin a badge on and lean against a bar, he'd be rewarded eventually with tips on anybody who'd ever been wanted for anything. Buy me a drink, buddy, and I'll tell you where you can find that dirty murdering so-and-so John Wilkes Booth. Cain. Benedict Arnold. Oops, Longarm thought, Arnold had been just a traitor, not a murderer. Well, no matter. You could get tips about that kind, too. Whatever you wanted to hear, never mind the facts.

With rare and fully reasoned exception, unsolicited tips were cheerfully ignored.

On the other hand, Vernal was close to where the new Ute reservation was being opened.

And if a federal officer had to be in the neighborhood anyway, why, there wasn't any reason why he shouldn't say hello to an acquaintance in passing. Lawyer Able, for instance.

"I, uh, reckon you want me to look into this Clete Bacon thing, Billy?"

6

"It crossed my mind."

"And if I need a horse or any other kind o' help, I maybe should ask at this new army post over there?"

"You know how upset the accounting office gets if we hire transportation or quarters when there are government facilities available locally."

Longarm smiled. Hell, this was interesting enough that he wasn't thinking about the sourness in his belly any longer. Besides, it was late enough he could wait until tomorrow to start west. He'd be feeling much better by then.

"I'll look into it," he said.

"You can find Lawyer Able at the Bradley House in Green River, Longarm."

"Thanks. I'll look for, um, him there." Longarm stood and went to the door. He was halfway through it when Billy called him back.

"Yes, boss?"

Billy was smiling that smile again. If he'd been a cat, Longarm would have looked for telltale feathers around his chops. "One thing more, Longarm."

"Yeah?"

"I gave you every opportunity to correct me. Is there something you haven't been telling me, Longarm?"

"I don't follow your meaning there, boss."

The smile grew wider. "On one of those telegrams I got back today, Longarm?"

"What about it?"

"The signature wasn't the usual A.B. on that one."

"No?"

"It was signed Agnes Able."

"Well, I'll be damned." Longarm shook his head in wonder. "Funny how sometimes the damnedest things will escape your notice, huh?" He scuttled the rest of the way out before Billy had time to react.

Behind him he could hear the marshal's laughter.

Chapter 2

Longarm was feeling much better by the time a Union Pacific westbound deposited him in Green River, Wyoming. Of course, by then he'd had well over twenty-four hours in which to recuperate after he left Billy Vail's office. The distance from Denver to Green River wasn't all that great by modern standards. After all, what was a few hundred miles when steam-driven engines could race tirelessly across the plains at thirty, even forty miles per hour of travel. On the other hand, getting from Denver to Green River required first that a man take one rail line east before he could finally connect with the Union Pacific and begin rolling west. By the time Longarm carried his gear into the lobby of the Bradley House, it was past nine o'clock in the evening, and the restaurant was already closing.

"I'd like a room, please. With a bath?"

The desk clerk gave Long a critical inspection, not saying anything, exactly, but managing to give the impression that he was detecting a faint odor, like a man taking a second sniff at the neck of a milk bottle left too long in the sun. "All of our rooms are equipped with bathing facilities. We find that ladies and *gentle*men prefer it so." The emphasis was strong enough to be unmistakable, slight enough there wasn't a damn thing Longarm could do about it. This desk clerk had snobby nastiness down cold, near to being an art. It wasn't an ability Longarm particularly admired.

"Well, now, ain't that right convenient," Longarm drawled. "How 'bout that." He reached for the guest register.

"Our rooms rent for three dollars," the clerk said with a sneer, obviously expecting the price to drive Longarm away.

"That so?" Longarm scrawled his name on the next open line, then took a moment to page back through the book. Aggie's distinctive handwriting was several lines above Longarm's. The signature of a Major Donald Benhurst was two pages back. Benhurst was the officer who may, or may not, have been murdered by the Ute scout Bird Talks to the Moon.

The hotel register, in fact, showed a Major and Mrs. Donald Benhurst. Billy hadn't mentioned anything about the widow Benhurst. Longarm couldn't help but wonder what light she might be able to shed on the deal, if any. He glanced through the guest register again and saw that Mrs. Benhurst had checked out when her husband did, so he wouldn't bother looking for her here.

"Are you quite through with my book, sir?" the clerk asked in a snippy, impatient tone.

"No, I reckon I ain't through with it quite yet," Longarm said blandly and continued to study the pages. Not that there was anything more to learn from them. The Bradley House was too rich a joint for many of the folks Longarm might know. For most army officers, too, he saw when he went through the names. Benhurst was the only military man shown since this register was started more than four months previously. Longarm thought that was kinda interesting even if it wasn't likely significant of anything. He yawned.

"You did hear me mention the room rate, did you not?" the clerk asked when Longarm pushed the book back across the counter to him.

Longarm smiled broadly, reached across the counter, and lightly patted the fellow on the cheek. "Be a nice boy now, hmm? Fetch my things t' my room an' draw me up that bath. An' after you done that, you can have me a supper sent t' my room, all right?"

"The restaurant is closed now, sir."

"Yeah, I seen that. That's why I say you should have something carried t' my room. Steak, o' course, cooked all the way done. You make sure o' that, hear, 'cause I like it plenty done. Spuds to go with that. Yeast rolls. Plenty butter. Pot o' coffee. An' I think some peach pie for a sweet."

"But—"

"Mind the pie is served nice an' warm. You'll have t' take it back an' heat it over if it ain't warm when I set to it. Top that all off with a bottle o' rye whiskey. Maryland distilled, now, none o' this New York State horsepiss. It's gotta be Maryland."

"But—"

"Now, sonny, you can't be listening to me if you're talking. So shut yourself up an' pay attention. After my meal's been delivered, you shake yourself around t' Miss Agnes Able's room an' present my compliments t' the lady. You do all that chop-chop, little fella, an' there might could be a whole dime in it just for you," Longarm said with a wicked smile that he sure as hell hoped the prissy prick would take every bit as insulting as Longarm intended it to be.

The clerk turned red in the jowls and commenced to sputter and fume.

Longarm snapped his fingers and said, "Chop-chop, sonny. Don't keep me waiting here."

"You didn't!" Aggie squealed happily.

Longarm gave her a modest aw-shucks grin and a nod.

"No wonder he was so red in the face when he came to my room," she said. "He was perfectly livid, but of course I didn't know why." Aggie, it turned out, didn't care for the Bradley House clerk a lick more than Longarm did.

The two of them were in her room now after an exchange of messages by way of the unhappy clerk, who seemed to feel himself above such errands even if he was being required to perform them tonight.

"I wish I could have heard it all for myself," she said.

"Not that much t' hear."

"He really did everything you said?"

"Hot pie an' everything. It was carried up so hot it was still most too warm t' enjoy by the time I got around t' eating it."

"And he supervised pouring the bathwater, too?"

"In person."

"Who must he think you are?"

Longarm grinned. "I never told him no lies on the subject. Was real careful not to."

"But who must he *think*?"

"Whoever or whatever, that's kinda his problem, ain't it?"

Aggie laughed again and wriggled a little closer to him on the settee they were sharing. Longarm knew it was inevitable

10

that he would have to give in to her before the night was done. She was being plenty obvious about what she had in mind, and it would be downright insulting for him to refuse her. But he did hope he could postpone it at least a little while longer. Agnes Able was a luscious redhead with flesh like sweetened cream and a figure that could have served as a model for the sexiest bar-wall painting ever put onto canvas. She was also a depressingly lousy fuck who simply didn't know enough about the subject of sex to recognize her faults.

She leaned closer, the warmth of her tits pressing against his arm, and she began to idly tickle and toy along the inside of his right thigh.

Longarm coughed into his fist. "Look, uh, before we, um, take up where we was before . . . if you know what I mean . . . could you tell me something more 'bout why you wanted me over here? I mean, me and my boss can't see that we got jurisdiction over this Bird Talks to the Moon fella. Not if he's a scout enrolled on the army books, we don't, 'cause then the case is purely military. An' they sure haven't shown any signs o' asking the Justice Department for help with it.

"Are you sure you don't want to talk business in the morning, dear?" Her face, undeniably pretty, was within inches of his now. Her breath was warm on his skin. Her eyes were huge. Open. Trusting.

Longarm felt, in fact, like something of a shit for wishing he could think of some way out of this.

Which didn't keep him from silently wishing for some way out of it.

Her hand found his and guided it to her breast. He could feel her heart beating wildly under his touch.

She took his other hand and brought it beneath the hem of her dressing gown. She was wearing nothing underneath the gown. He could feel the moist heat of her even before his fingers found the soft curls that crowned her mound.

Aggie groaned when he touched her. She tensed and became rigid, and her breathing quickened just from that small contact. One good finger wiggle, he knew, and she would reach the first of many explosions. She was that quick and easy to be triggered.

11

What the hell. He found the spot he wanted and rubbed it gently. Aggie stiffened, gasped, then seemed to melt as a jolt of raw pleasure burst through her.

What a stinking shame, he thought, that she should be built so loose and sloppy that she couldn't give back anything like the pleasure she was able to take with a man. And was so prudish on the subject, despite her horny actions, that she wasn't interested in learning any of the other ways it would have been possible for her to please a man.

Screwing Aggie was basically an exercise in futility, as he'd come to learn in the past.

Still, he was determined to be pleasant and friendly no matter what.

He gave her a deep, penetrating kiss while lightly touching her crotch. He felt the tiny, convulsive little explosions ripple through her body as she responded far out of proportion to what he was doing.

Such a waste, he thought regretfully even as he poked and prodded and brought her to one trembling climax after another.

Chapter 3

Longarm reached for the bowl of scrambled eggs and emptied the rest of it onto his plate. Aggie was already done with her breakfast, but he was still unsatisfied. There seemed to be a lot of that going around lately.

Oh, he'd managed to get it off once or twice during the night. But he'd sure as hell had to work to accomplish that much. And he hadn't ever been completely satisfied.

There might not've been anything he could have done about that last night, but he could sure do something about this other kind of hunger over the breakfast Aggie'd had brought up to her room. He polished off the last of the eggs, took the last few slices of bacon, and damn near finished the basket of fresh biscuits, too.

"Hand me that jelly, please."

She passed the jar to him and poured coffee for both of them. "Will you be leaving for Fort Brunot today?"

"That's where they're keeping Bird Talks to the Moon?" He slathered a biscuit thick with butter and then piled strawberry jam onto it.

"You didn't know that?"

"Aggie, it might amaze you how damn little I know 'bout this case. Billy only had what information was in your telegrams. An' last night you claimed you was too busy t' talk about it."

"Oh, dear."

He grunted and reached for his coffee cup. The coffee was as good as everything else had proved to be. A man could get himself spoiled to the kind of treatment he received at a fancy place like this Bradley House. They say money won't buy happiness, and Longarm was willing to accept that that

13

was true. On the other hand, it looked like money would allow a fella to be miserable in real comfort.

"Let me fill you in, dear," Aggie offered.

Longarm grunted again. He finally felt replete, so he leaned back and reached for a cheroot. Aggie was already smoking. Since he'd seen her last, she'd changed from smoking small cigars, which she'd probably started doing only as a way of snubbing her nose at the conventional ways of doing things, and now had taken up smoking cigarettes, a habit that seemed to be catching on in some quarters lately with men and some women, too.

"Now," he said. "Tell me everything you know 'bout this, if you please. An' in particular I want t' know how you figure a deputy marshal can claim jurisdiction in a matter that clearly belongs t' the army an' not us."

Longarm stepped out into the bright glare of the morning sunshine. He tilted his Stetson to the side to keep it out of his eyes and ambled down the street toward the railroad depot. While he walked he mulled over what Aggie'd told him.

It was one weak and shaky kind of hook she was trying to hang a case on here.

What it came down to was that nobody knew shit about what Bird Talks to the Moon—Talking Bird she called him, but then Aggie wasn't one to worry over details like getting an Indian's name straight; somehow she just couldn't get a handle on most of them—did or did not do in connection with the death of this Major Donald Benhurst and his two-man escort.

The Ute, including the other Ute scouts, hadn't been allowed to speak with Bird Talks since the day he'd been arrested. And the United States Army wasn't saying a damn thing on the subject, not to her or to the Ute elders or to anybody else, either. They clammed up and remained completely mum on the subject of Benhurst and about Bird Talks, too.

Aggie's request to the Justice Department was really a fishing expedition on her part. Since nobody really knew what Bird Talks was charged with, or if he'd been charged with anything, or if he was gonna be charged with anything, she reasoned that he was being held without due process. That was, she claimed,

14

a violation of Section 1 of the Fourteenth Amendment to the Constitution.

"You're reaching. You know that, don't you?"

"Dammit, Longarm, if Indians are entitled to habeas corpus protections, they're entitled to all the other constitutional guarantees as well. The courts can't pick and choose which freedoms to protect and which to ignore. In for a penny, then in for a pound, dear."

"Just for the sake o' argument let's say that your theory holds up an' that the court will someday rule that Indians do have all the same rights as anybody else, all the way down t' buying guns and whiskey—"

"Of course they should. Why—"

"Whoa, now. I already said we'll assume that it's exactly like you say, so don't be giving me no speeches. Save all that for a judge when it someday has t' be decided."

"All right." She sounded reluctant as hell to let go of her zeal on the subject, but she did set it aside for the moment.

"My point is that since you don't know what's happening to this Bird Talks fella, you don't know that his rights ain't being protected."

"And my point," she countered, "is that *you* don't know that they *are*."

"So you want me t' just waltz in at this Fort Brunot place an' start throwing my weight around, even though I got no claim to jurisdiction *unless* I can show violation of these Fourteenth Amendment protections. Which, by the way, haven't yet been ruled valid in any court in this entire land. Is that about the size of it?"

"Darling," she'd said quite happily, "you know I wouldn't ask you to do that. Not on the *surface*, I wouldn't."

"Not on the surface," he'd repeated dryly.

Aggie had reached over and squeezed his hand. "Really, dear. We both know that you are a perfectly wonderful peace officer. And more than a bit of a finagler, too. I don't expect you to do anything obvious. But I have every confidence that you will find some way to accomplish what I want. After all, dear, that's why I suggested that Wet Horse ask the Justice Department for your help."

"You suggested it," he said.

15

"That's right. Which as the band's attorney I had every right to do. Every duty to do, in fact, if I expect to represent their best interests."

"And you suggested this t' some fella called Wet Horse?"

"Surely you know him. He said you do. Wet Horse is headman of the northern lizard clan or some such. I never can get all that straight in my mind."

"Lizard." It took him a moment to make the connection. Then he chuckled and nodded. "Yeah, I know him." Aggie, as usual, hadn't gotten the name quite right. The old sonofabitch was Pissing Horse. He was a thief, a scoundrel, a liar of great accomplishment. Longarm liked the old fart enormously. And liked one of Pissing Horse's granddaughters even more. Yeah, he knew Aggie's "Wet Horse" all right. "Jeez, I'm surprised the old bastard is still alive."

"Alive enough to pretend to have a coughing fit so he could lean on me and feel me up."

"That sounds like him, all right."

"Well, he's the one who officially is making the request to the Justice Department for your help."

"That won't do you no good if I got no jurisdiction. You know that."

"I also think we can . . . well, just between you, me, and the gatepost, dear, I would admit that I'm hoping we can create a claim for jurisdiction in the matter. I'll leave it up to you how you do it."

"This Fourteenth Amendment thing is thin."

"Whatever works, dear. If that is all you can give me to work with, why, I'll file an action asking the court to implement it."

"That'd have t' go all the way to the Supreme Court. Could take years t' shake out."

"And if it does, dear, I shall have my client free under bond and the army on the defensive until it is resolved. It won't be my Ute who have to react, because I'll be the one on the offense."

"Hell, Aggie, I almost believe you could do it, too." Bad as she was in bed, the woman was no slouch when it came to writing a legal brief, as she'd proved with her Nebraska filings during that other case. As a lawyer, woman or no, she was plenty sharp.

16

All of that had been upstairs in the Bradley House. Aggie had laid out a campaign based mostly on bluster and bullshit and was counting on Deputy Custis Long to go out and make it work.

Now it was up to him to see if her faith was misplaced or not.

Which might not be so damned easy to do.

Chapter 4

"No, sir, I'm sorry, he isn't here. I haven't seen him since, oh, sometime day before yesterday. That morning, I think it was, because I don't recall seeing him when I came back from my dinner. He hadn't said anything about leaving, though. I would have remembered if he did."

"Is it unusual for him to stay away like this?"

"Sure is. Six days a week, seven in the morning to five in the evening, he's generally here. Not at his key the whole time, you understand, but close enough to hear if there's traffic coming in on the army line," the civilian telegrapher at the Green River railroad depot said.

"Is there a backup man who comes in on the regular man's days off, anybody monitoring the key at night, anything like that?"

The response was a shake of the head to each of those. "Nobody else, mister. Major communications points stay open day and night because of the railroad's train orders, but even we shut down at night here, at least so far as commercial traffic is concerned. The army closes nights and Sundays."

"Where could I find his superiors?" Longarm asked. "Or is there an army detachment in town now?"

"No post here," the helpful telegrapher said, "but there's a quartermaster outfit that's supposed to see to the off-loading of government supplies and arrange transportation to wherever the stuff is supposed to go next. I've seen a sergeant and two men . . . slick operators all three of them, if you want my opinion; I'd say they wrangled this deal on purpose and got them something extra going on the side . . . and there's a pigeon-puffy lieutenant supposed to be in charge of the others. I suppose Johnny—he's the operator here, Corporal

18

John Myer—I suppose he fits in with the quartermaster bunch somehow. Not that he has all that much to do with any of them that I've noticed. In his free time, I mean. Johnny's married and doesn't go in much for gambling and carousing like those quartermaster enlisted men do. I don't think he ever sees much of them on duty or off. The lieutenant, he stops in a couple times a day to check on the message traffic. I'd say that Johnny is mostly on his own here. He just does what he's supposed to and goes home to his wife. They, uh, only been married a few months." The telegrapher winked.

"Thanks for all your help."

"Any time."

Longarm started for the door, paused, then turned back. "You don't happen to know where the corporal and his bride are living, do you?"

"Sure thing." The civilian gave clear, sensible directions, then concluded, "If they don't answer right away, mister, wait a little extra. Takes some time to get dressed in the middle of the day, you know."

Longarm laughed and said goodbye.

He found it decidedly odd that the army's telegraph key would be left unattended now. Of course, it didn't necessarily follow that Billy Vail's inquiries about Bird Talks to the Moon had anything to do with that. Even though none of those messages was ever answered. And even though that same time is about when the army key was shut down. It didn't *necessarily* follow. Sure.

Longarm grimaced and lighted a cheroot.

A few words with Corporal Myer might just provide a whole lot of illumination on that subject. And Longarm would sure like to have at least a little more knowledge before he showed up at the gate of this Fort Brunot place. Wherever the hell it was.

He followed the telegraph operator's directions and found the Myer house without once getting lost. Confused two or three times but never actually lost. It turned out to be a tiny, clapboard house set cheek by jowl with a whole bunch of others just like it, all of them arranged in a small cul-de-sac that was serviced by a common well. It was the sort of neighborhood that would all be owned by one landlord and rented out on the cheap. At least the landlord here wasn't any penny-pinching price gouger. From what Longarm could see, he kept the places in good repair. The walls and roofs seemed tight and protective, and the trim on each place was painted a different bright color to give a semblance of individuality to the houses, red on the door and window frames of one place, blue on another, yellow and green and white and so on.

Apparently, the people who rented here were young married couples, decent working folks. A clothes-drying rack set near the central well was hung thick with diaper cloths, and some-one had erected a makeshift teeter-totter nearby. Toddlers and small children up to the age of five or thereabouts played on the front stoops of the miniature houses, and he could hear the wailing protests of more than one infant coming through open windows on all sides.

The newly married Myers were said to live in a place with green trim that had a rocking chair on the porch. There were two places that fit the description, but one of them had a collection of homemade toys tumbled into a box beside the rocker. So the newlyweds pretty much had to live in the other one. Longarm rapped loudly on the door—closed, even though most of the houses were left open on this fair day—and waited patiently for a response.

"Mister?" The woman's voice came from behind him.

Longarm turned and removed his Stetson. "Yes, ma'am?" The woman—she seemed little more than a girl, actually, but the babe suckling at her breast beneath a hastily draped shawl said she was a woman now—was slim and pale and pretty. Even though she had come out onto the stoop of the house next door, she was only a few feet away.

"You looking for Johnny and Meg, mister?"

"I'm looking for Corporal Myer, yes."

The lady's eyes narrowed in suspicion. "You ain't a friend of theirs?"

"No, I haven't had the pleasure of meeting them yet," he said.

"You ain't army, neither."

Longarm smiled. "No, I'm not."

"You don't look like you're a salesman."

"No, ma'am."

The young woman gave him a look of sheer exasperation. "Mister, I'm running out of things you don't look like. Am I gonna have to come right out and ask you?"

Longarm laughed. "I'm an employee of the government. I'm supposed to interview Corporal Myer about his job." None of which was any sort of a lie. Not the truth, either, of course.

"A dang paper pusher," the girl complained. She looked disappointed.

"Yes, ma'am, I'm afraid so. Although if I'm lucky they'll give me a promotion soon and I can count pencils instead of pushing papers. That pays a whole lot better, you know."

She grinned and tossed her head, flinging the hair out of her face. The movement momentarily disrupted the slurping and cooing of the baby at her breast. The noisy little bugger had a hearty appetite. "You'll have to come ask your questions some other time, Mister Paper Pusher. Johnny and Meg are off on a trip."

"Really? I'm sorry to hear that."

"Yeah, he got some time off, and some friend of his over at the train station gave him a couple railroad passes. Meg's mother lives in Nebraska someplace. That's where they've went."

"You don't happen t' know when they'll be back?"

"No, I sure don't. Don't think they know for sure themselves. It was kinda like Johnny wouldn't be needed for a while, so they could go off till he got called back. Meg woulda told me all about it except it happened real sudden. We hardly got to talk at all before they were packed and out of here. There was a train they could catch if they hurried."

"Lucky fella," Longarm said.

"I sure wish my man would be so lucky. Haven't seen my folks in almost two years. And if Leroy don't let me take a rest from having children soon, I don't expect I'll live long enough to get all the way back to Ohio. The nasty little brats are turning me old before my time." She was caressing the baby's back with tender care even as she said that and obviously meant not a word of it.

"As young and lovely as you are, ma'am, I'm sure you can look forward to a happy reunion someday." Longarm bowed

21

gallantly. "And if I may say so, your husband is quite a lucky man himself."

"Go on with you now," she protested with a simper and a blush. But she sounded pleased.

"Thanks for your help, ma'am," Longarm said with a smile as he donned his Stetson again and turned away.

He wasn't smiling inside, though.

It was strange, damned strange, that an army corporal should be given free time of unspecified duration. And following immediately on the heels of Marshal Vail's inquiries, too.

The implication clearly was that the army had something to hide. Longarm wished it was equally clear what that something was. And why.

He scowled and headed back toward town in search of the quartermaster detachment.

Surely they couldn't have been dismissed from their duties, too. Not considering the huge volumes of stores and equipment required to establish a new army post and a new Indian reservation. All of that would be moving through Green River now, and someone would have to be here to take charge of it.

No, Longarm felt confident that he would be able to find the quartermaster people here.

Then, dammit, he should get some answers.

Chapter 5

"No, sir, I'm sorry. I haven't seen them since, oh, yesterday? I think it was yesterday."

Longarm's scowl deepened. The Fort Brunot quartermaster detachment billeted in Green River occupied second-story office space above a hardware store close to the Union Pacific tracks.

That much had been easy enough to determine.

But now the owner of the hardware store was giving him very much the same story he'd gotten from that telegraph operator. Yes, they should normally be here. No, they weren't around at the moment. Damn!

"No idea where they've gone or why?"

The man shrugged. "None of my business, mister. All I know is that I was paid in advance for the rent. Six months' worth. Until the rent comes due again, I don't care if I never see another soldier."

Longarm's interest quickened. If this man had a complaint about the men from Fort Brunot, it might give some hints about the rest of this odd behavior. He leaned forward and in a confidential tone of voice posed the question.

"Oh, not really. Those enlisted men peeve me sometimes. Not about anything they do here, mind. It's just that two of them run a three-card monte game in their off time, and the sergeant comes along behind and loansharks money to the victims. The young fella who works for me got sucked into that. Twenty percent interest. Per damned month! It's an old racket. Let me tell you, I gave my helper a talking to and then another just like it to those soldiers. They've left my people alone since then. Wish I could say as much for the poor saps they take on payday nights."

Longarm was disappointed. Six-for-five loan enterprises were virtually a tradition in the army, and if they weren't exactly honorable, they weren't very far from it, either. As for the monte game, well, anybody who wanted to take the risk was entitled. There is no law against stupidity.

"Even the lieutenant is gone?" he asked the hardware store owner.

"Friend, I don't claim that any one of them has gone anyplace. Only that I haven't seen any of them go up and down those stairs since yesterday sometime."

"Thank you, sir. I appreciate your help."

Longarm left the store and went back to the Union Pacific depot. He stopped in at the telegraph office.

"Freight master? Sure," the operator told him. "That would be Hands Curtis."

"Hans?"

The telegrapher grinned. "No, sir. Hands. But don't call him that to his face unless you're wanting a scrap to get you some exercise. Call him Mr. Curtis and act polite and he'll do anything he can to help you. There isn't a train in right now, so you'll probably find him in the UP offices behind the passenger lobby. There or in the Milwaukee Saloon across the street."

"Thanks."

There wasn't anyone in the railroad offices at the moment. Even the ticket window was closed. A pasteboard sign had been propped in the opening to say Back in 10. Longarm reversed course and headed for the Milwaukee.

Once he was inside, he didn't even have to ask anyone which customer would be Hands Curtis. A huge bear of a man standing at the end of the bar had to be the man in question. Like many large men he had thick, powerfully built, oversize hands. But that wasn't where the nickname came from.

At first glance Longarm had thought this man was wearing fur gloves on a warm day. Then he realized. Curtis's hands were covered so thick with black hair it looked like fur. Except for his palms being pale and not particularly leathery, the man might have borrowed his hands from an ape. Longarm figured it was no wonder the poor fellow was sensitive about it.

24

"Mr. Curtis?"

"Yeah?"

"Could I ask you a few questions?"

"Why?"

Longarm gave him a disarming smile. "Because I want the answers, of course."

Hands Curtis chuckled. "Ask away, friend."

Longarm did.

"Sure, they talked to me, oh, it was a couple nights ago. Said they had to report back to the post. Didn't say why, just that they had to go back for a spell. I'm supposed to point out the army stuff to the teamsters, and they'll take it from there. You could call it supervision of goods past delivery and none of my business, but what the hell. The way I see it, the army does a lot of business with the railroad, and it isn't any big thing. It won't take me but a few minutes of my time, and a fella always likes to build up some favors."

"Goods are still moving through for Brunot, then?" Longarm said.

"Oh, sure. I see the freight schedules, you know. There's plenty of stuff consigned for Brunot every week. Two, sometimes three trains of freight wagons to haul it all. Food, clothes, building materials, furniture, stoves, kitchen equipment, hospital equipment, boilers, and laundry facilities, all kinds of stuff. You wouldn't believe what all it takes to make a fort. At least, I wouldn't have believed it if I hadn't seen all these bills of lading. It only makes sense once you think about it, though. It's like they're starting from scratch and putting up a whole new town."

"I hadn't thought of it like that, but you're right."

"Yes, sir, indeed I am."

"Could I buy you a beer, Hands?"

The nickname slipped out before Longarm had time to think and to stop it from sliding off his damned tongue.

The problem was that he'd first been told about this man by the nickname, then warned against using it. Dammit, why hadn't the telegrapher just avoided it altogether.

Now it was too late. Now the damage was done.

Curtis's eyes went wide, and he stiffened just a little.

25

Aw, shit, Longarm figured. And such a big'un. Longarm quite frankly wasn't sure if he could take this guy with his bare, unfurry hands or not.

Which was not to say that he wasn't willing to make the attempt. Once Curtis threw the first punch, well, there wouldn't be time for explanations then.

And anyway, dammit, Longarm wasn't fixing to grovel. Not to anybody. Not on any subject. He'd gone and made the mistake, but his only regret was if he'd given offense. That he would be sorry for. Nothing else. Longarm stiffened, too, prepared to dart clear if the fur commenced to fly.

"Hands?" Curtis repeated.

Longarm kept his face impassive.

Curtis threw his head back and laughed. "By Godfrey, mister, you're the first man in ages with honesty enough to say in front of me what everybody else whispers behind me. How's about I buy you a beer instead?"

Longarm would have had to admit to some feelings of relief as he propped an elbow on the bar beside Hands Curtis and nodded his acceptance of the offer.

"You bet," he said and with a wink added, "if you let me provide the refills."

"You're all right, mister." Hands motioned for the bartender.

Chapter 6

Hands Curtis did much more than buy Longarm a beer. The Union Pacific's big freight master also provided him with a ride to Fort Brunot.

When Hands heard that his new friend needed information that would only be available at the fort, he quickly volunteered to help.

"I got three wagons starting out for Brunot first thing tomorrow morning. The shipment they're to carry is due in tonight. My boys will load it out of the cars to the platform, and the teamsters will take it from there. They won't pull out till daybreak, though, just load and park till they have light to travel by."

"Will there be an army officer with the wagons?" Longarm asked, still hoping to find someone official in town so he could start getting the answers he needed.

"Nope. These teamsters are contract employees. They're paid by the army but not mustered."

Longarm grunted.

"Be glad to put you aboard as a passenger. Wouldn't be no charge for it. They owe me plenty of favors."

"Is there a quicker way I could get there, Hands?"

"Might be one, Longarm, but I don't know of it. There's civilians at a town called Vernal. That ain't too far from Brunot. But there's no regular coach schedule from here down to there. I dunno, maybe you could take the train on to Salt Lake and see if you can find fast passage back east to Vernal. Or maybe not. I wouldn't know. The wagons, they'll take just under four days. And that's if there's no serious breakdown. Be there middle of the afternoon on the fourth day if everything goes normal. It's the best I know to tell you."

27

"Thanks, Hands. I'll do it your way."

Bird Talks to the Moon would just have to sit patient in his cell—if he was indeed in a cell; that was among the many things Aggie hadn't been clear on—until then.

As for the immediate future, as in this particular afternoon while waiting for the shipment of Fort Brunot goods to arrive, well, Longarm couldn't think of anything much better than to stand here at the bar of the Milwaukee and have a few more drinks with his very good friend Hands Curtis.

"My turn t' buy, Hands."

"Are you sure?"

"Pretty sure."

"I think it's my turn, Longarm."

"Shit, let's both buy."

"I should've thought of that myself."

"Bartender! Two more rounds here."

Longarm weaved only a little bit coming down the stairs. The night was still young—well, close to being young—and there was yet some fun to be had. To be on the safe side, though, he was checking out of the hotel now and throwing his gear into the back of the freight rig that would be his home for the next few days. The teamsters and their helpers turned out to be just as nice as Longarm's good pal ol' Hands. He had confidence in them, sure they would pour him into the back of the wagon, too, if that was what was necessary come the dawning. Until then he could let his hair down and relax for a change.

He plunked his McClellan onto the counter, scabbarded Winchester and all, and grinned at the desk clerk's horrified expression. Shit, a body would think a fella could set his gear down without all that much fuss. The buckles and the stirrup irons weren't causing that much damage. Why, those little bitty scratches wouldn't show at all hardly once the countertop was polished a mite.

Longarm belched. The desk clerk glared.

Longarm grinned. The desk clerk sniffed.

"Checking out, sir?"

"You don't hafta look s' damned happy about it."

"I'm sure I don't know what you mean. Are you checking out or not, sir?"

"Yeah, I'm checking out."

"You realize that I shall have to charge you for tonight. You are long past our normal check-out time."

"You do that," Longarm suggested. There were other suggestions he might have liked to make to this particular individual. He was right proud of himself for keeping all of those quiet.

"That will be six dollars in room charges for the two nights, sir. Plus . . . let me see here. . . ." He rummaged through a small file box and brought out several slips of paper. "Room service, hot water, umm, the total for your stay, sir, would be eleven dollars and forty cents. Plus gratuities. Shall I calculate those for you, sir?"

Longarm smiled. He'd already tipped the boy who carried his supper up last night and the one who'd brought breakfast to Aggie's room this morning. Far as he could see that was all the gratuities there needed to be. Or anyway, all there was going to be. He sure as hell wasn't intending to make any deposits onto the open palm of this snotty S.O.B.

"I reckon I can manage," he said. He pulled out a government expense voucher and laid it on the counter. "Mind if I borrow that pen? Thanks." He plucked the pen out of the clerk's fingers and filled out the appropriate boxes on the voucher slip, then signed it and shoved both pen and paper across to the clerk. "Here."

"Sir? You've made a mistake. See here? You filled this in wrong."

"Are you sure?" Longarm blinked and leaned close. He gave the voucher an owlish inspection, belched loudly, and nodded. "Looks right t' me."

"But this authorizes payment of only a dollar fifty. Do you want to pay the remainder in cash, is that it?"

"No, I'd say that's right. You told me last night that the room rate is three dollars. Which I agreed to. Three dollars a week, that's fifty cents a night. Two nights, that's the dollar. Then another fifty cents for supper. Dollar and a half total. And I done tipped that boy last night already, so you needn't worry 'bout him."

"But—"

"You can count on me tellin' all my friends 'bout what a nice place you have here." Longarm retrieved his things and stumbled out into the night.

Time was wasting, dammit, and there were people to talk to, drinks to get down, a bit of fun to be had before those wagons pulled out in the morning.

It didn't occur to him until much, much later that he had left Green River without remembering to tell Aggie where he was going.

Chapter 7

"Why are we stopping, Joey?"

"You said you wanted a look at the place where those soldier boys was murdered, didn't you? Well, this is it."

Longarm nodded and climbed down off the bed of the massive freight rig. The wagon was twice as tall as a Conestoga and had a cargo box at least four times as spacious as that of one of the elegant but essentially inefficiently covered outfits that really had been designed for use in Pennsylvania and Ohio. Hell, Joey Dunfrey's mule-drawn wagon pulled a trailer that was bigger than a Conestoga.

The other two wagons stopped behind Joey's, and everybody piled out for a chance to walk and stretch a little.

There were six teamsters along, one driver and one helper for each rig. The driver handled the mules by way of a single jerk line attached to the headstall of the lead mule, far forward in the twelve-up hitches. The helper's main job was to keep the axle bearings greased and, at night or during extended layovers, the wheel spokes moist to ensure against the shrinkage that would lead to busted wagon wheels.

As soon as the wagons stopped, each driver saw that his mules were secured, and each helper grabbed his grease pot and daubing stick, the drivers scurrying forward along their hitches and the helpers ducking underneath the massive freight boxes to lubricate the running gear. It was an efficient and by now entirely commonplace sequence of events so far as Longarm was concerned.

Over the past three days he had gotten to know the teamsters fairly well. They were a likable bunch, energetic and honest if not particularly bright or witty.

They gave him their full approval in return. Longarm sus-

31

pected that had something to do with the fact that sometime during their last night in Green River they'd talked him into buying a two-gallon crock of trade whiskey to contribute to the supplies for the journey.

That right there had been popular enough. He'd compounded their approval by discovering that the horsepiss was too horrid to drink unless a man was already pretty well shot to start with. At least, in Longarm's opinion, it was. The teamsters didn't necessarily share that notion and were delighted to discover that the whiskey would only have to be shared six ways instead of seven. Longarm's contribution to the general good had lasted into their second night on the road.

Now, in the last day before they reached Fort Brunot, they were on a little-traveled cutoff that angled away from the main road. The more busily traveled north-south road ran parallel to and west of the Green, far above its confluence with the Colorado to become one of the great and mighty rivers of the country. Up this far north the Green wasn't much shakes.

The road, or so Longarm was told, ran on south through Vernal on the Utah side of the river and connected by ferry with Brown's Hole on the Colorado side.

Here, though, miles were saved by angling southwest to the new Ute Indian reservation and accompanying army post.

It was along this dry and lonely strip, Joey explained, that the murders had taken place.

"Hell, yes, I know 'bout them, Longarm," he'd said. "That was the biggest excitement in this country since Lame Tom Hollister caught his Mary in the milking shed with John Applegate. An' let me tell you, 'twasn't no cow's teat she was milking 'at day." He winked. "An' not her hands she was usin' for the job of it, neither."

"Somehow I must've missed hearing about that one," Longarm confessed.

"Old Tom, he took a pitchfork to 'em. They didn't see him coming in, bein' otherwise occupied, if you see what I mean, so he up and walks in behind 'em and jabs. Got the both of them at the same time, Applegate in the nuts and Mary, well, you get the idea."

"Yeah, I suppose I do."

"Those soldier boys being outright murdered, and by wild

Indians at that, that was the most excitement this country's maybe ever had," Joey said with a tone that smacked of eagerness to know more.

"What happened to those other people?" Longarm asked. "Applegate and . . . What'd you say the others' names were?"

"John Applegate, he recovered, but I've heard it said that he can't get a hard-on no more after taking a steel pitchfork tine up the old wazoo. Mary Hollister, she took sick and died a little after that business in the milk shed."

"And her husband?"

Joey looked as if he didn't know what Longarm was getting at with the question. "Lame Tom? What about him?"

"Did he go to trial? Hang? Get off? What?"

"What would he go to trial for?"

"Assault, for one thing."

"Shit, John wasn't gonna have it dragged out in public 'bout him getting his gonads ventilated with another man's manure fork."

"But the woman, dammit. You just said she died."

"Sure, but Tom didn't kill her. I told you, she took sick an' died."

"Of what? A festering puncture wound put there by her husband?" Longarm snapped.

"Jesus, man, I wouldn't know 'bout that. Nobody would. Nobody's gonna look under a woman's skirts t' see if her pussy is rotted away."

"Did the doctor—?"

"Don't got no doctor down here yet. Hell, Longarm, we don't hardly got no people down here. Way we see it, Mary took sick an' died, that's all. There's nothing t' say Tom had anything t' do with it."

Longarm grunted and let it be. It wasn't his problem to worry about. Thank goodness.

The murder of three soldiers, though, just might be.

And Joey and the other teamsters knew exactly where to find the place where Major Benhurst and his escort had been ambushed.

"You won't find no souvenirs, Longarm," Joey cautioned as he led the way from the wagons toward a dry arroyo. "We already looked."

33

"Thanks," Longarm said, his voice every bit as dry as the arroyo bed. He took a cheroot out and lighted it, then trailed along behind Joey Dunfrey. If he'd been hoping to learn anything from an undisturbed crime scene . . .

They stood on the rim overlooking the arroyo, and Joey pointed things out for Longarm's benefit.

"You can see the bloodstains there an' there an' there."

All three were at the bottom of the wash and on the side of it nearer the wagon road.

"That there one that's a little bit apart from the others? They say that one is where the major got his. Them other two would've been the sojers that was with him. You can't see nothing now, of course, but they tell me when they first found the bodies, they all of 'em had their flies unbuttoned and their whangs hanging out an' that there was damp spots like they'd all stopped to take a piss and that's what they was doing when they was shot down."

Longarm grunted again. With the major's lady seated in the carriage or ambulance or whatever . . . yeah, it would have made sense for the men to go down into the bottom of the arroyo to relieve themselves. There wasn't much else to get out of sight behind in this dry, mostly empty country. Hell, right here there weren't even sagebrush clumps taller than a man's boots, much less brush to go behind. An arroyo bottom would be about it.

So assume the soldiers all went down there together, officer and enlisted men alike, it would have given someone—Bird Talks to the Moon, presumably—an opportunity to come up on them.

Longarm turned and looked back toward the road. There was no way he could tell for sure where the Benhurst wagon would have been parked. But it was probably safe to say it would have been as close to the arroyo as possible. Call that thirty yards minimum, possibly more depending on the precise location where the driver came to a halt.

Between the road and this spot where Longarm now stood there wasn't any more cover to hide behind than a few wisps of desert grass.

"You don't know if the men were shot from front or back, do you?" he asked Joey.

"Front," the teamster said. "That's what was told t' me."

"And they were facing . . . ?"

"This way. I wasn't here, mind, but the fella I talked to was. He was one of them that had to carry the bodies to Brunot for burying. He told me all the details of it, me bein' interested kinda."

Joey's interest had been no more than morbid curiosity, a quality that Longarm recognized but never had understood although it was part and parcel of ordinary human nature. The same quality that at its lowest, meanest, cruelest, and most stupid form prompted parents to hold their small children up high so the kiddies could look over the crowds in front of them and see all the pretty scarlet gore where some woman had been run over by a wagon or some man had gotten his brains blown against a wall. Longarm never had understood why folks did that. Still, he was gonna take advantage of it now and pump Joey for all the man knew. Considering the way things were going so far, he might not get any better opportunities once he reached Fort Brunot.

He offered Joey a smoke and asked the leading questions and listened with unfeigned interest while the teamster related everything his soldier friend had told him.

Longarm absorbed it without comment except to add a question now and then so as to keep the flow of words going.

Finally he grunted and thanked the friendly teamster for his help.

"Sure thing, Longarm. Anything I can do. You know that."

"And I appreciate it, Joey. Now let's see if we can't make t the rest of the way in to Brunot this afternoon. I do believe I remember promising t' buy you boys a drink."

"Funny how that went an' slipped my mind," Joey said with a grin. "But I won't call you a liar, Longarm. Better I let you buy me that drink, eh?" He laughed and motioned for the others to return to the wagons.

35

Chapter 8

Whatever Longarm had been expecting to see at Fort Brunot . . . this wasn't it.

The freight wagons rolled out of the last swale and onto the barren, arid flat that held the encampment. Spread out before them was a collection of wind-whipped, weather-frayed tents in varying shapes and sizes, numerous heaps of native rock each at least the size of a man's head and each mound piled to just about head high, several wall-like stone structures that were no taller than knee high on a grown man . . . and one flagpole displaying the Stars and Stripes.

There wasn't a single actual building on the grounds yet, although post-and-string markers showed where foundations were being marked out, ready for construction.

The "stables" were no more than a picket line of stout rope where horses could be tied. Equipment was tossed in piles nearby and covered with tarpaulins. A poor-quality hay forage was stacked untidily around a rick pole and left uncovered.

The soldiers of Fort Brunot shifted about from here to there on slow-moving tasks, most of them stripped to the waist while they labored in the glare of the sunlight. But then, any outdoor activities here would require hot, strength-sapping effort. The countryside around Brunot was no desert, not by any stretch of the imagination, but it was no lush territory, either. For some reason the army post had been sited on a flat that was dry and brown and barren even though the terrain in view to the west was green and, at least in contrast, quite lovely. Longarm thought the choice of location here was . . . well . . . *shitty* was the term that came to mind.

"This is it?"

"Yeah, coming along pretty good, too, I'd say," Joey said around a mouthful of tobacco.

If this was pretty good, Longarm was just as happy he'd missed seeing the place when it was rough.

Joey guided his short train of wagons around behind all the activity to a group of low, loaf-shaped, tarpaulin-covered mounds. There were dozens of the small mounds, materials brought in on earlier trips, Longarm guessed, each wagonload of goods set on the ground and covered on the spot for storage against the time when those particular items would be needed. That was probably as good a system as any so long as someone knew what was on hand and where it might be located.

Several of the soldiers waved friendly greetings to Joey and the other teamsters, and by the time the wagons came to a halt, there was a corporal on hand to accept the bill of lading Dunfrey handed over. The corporal signed the freight company's copy and handed it back without bothering to inspect any of the materials the civilians were already unloading onto bare dirt. That casually endorsed piece of paper, Longarm suspected, was a certification that everything on the bill of lading was present and in good order. The signature would allow the freighters to be paid for their haulage.

And if some of the items were lost or broken en route from the railroad tracks, well, that would be the army's loss once the form was signed and handed over.

Lost. Or broken. Or stolen.

Not that Longarm had any reason to suspect Joey and his friends of anything like that. Far from it. Hell, he'd come to know them well over the past few days and liked them. But that didn't mean that everyone was honest. Basically, the tall deputy hated to see any way of doing things that allowed theft. This system at Brunot practically encouraged it. The army could be stolen blind here, and no one would ever figure it out because no one was bothering to compare the paperwork with the actual goods that were being dragged out of the wagons and dumped onto the ground.

The corporal took the army's copies of the paperwork and disappeared into a large tent that Longarm assumed would be the post headquarters. By then another man had come over to the wagons, this one a civilian. "Anything for me, Joe?"

"No, sir, not this trip, Mr. Roach." Dunfrey turned to Longarm and said, "This gentleman is the camp sutler, Longarm. We'll see him after we're done working an' collect those drinks you promised."

The sutler beamed and shoved a hand out to shake. "Mr. Longarm, is it? A pleasure, sir. You would be with the freight company, I take it? Indeed, a real pleasure."

Longarm winked at Joey over Roach's shoulder and didn't correct the man about that erroneous assumption. After all, who but a freight company employee would be riding on the freight wagons. And a boss of some level, too, to be dressed like Longarm was and not be taking part in the labor of unloading the wagons.

"I promised to buy the boys a round or two, Mr. Roach, so I'm sure we'll all see you shortly."

"My pleasure, Mr. Longarm. And my treat. Your money is no good with me tonight, sir, ha ha." Roach was so quick and oily with the offer that Longarm suspected he was up to something here, perhaps getting the benefit of low-price transport for his goods or possibly even finagling his freight costs free courtesy of an unknowing army paymaster.

Not that any of this was really a United States deputy marshal's worry. It wasn't for him or for Billy Vail to worry about even if Sutler Roach pocketed half the annual budget for the Department of the Army. Not until or unless the Department of the Army requested Justice Department assistance.

Longarm smiled and nodded and pulled out a cheroot. "See you later, Mr. Roach."

"I look forward to it, Mr. Longarm." Roach shook hands again and left in the direction of a pale tent set off by itself beyond the picket line.

"While you boys finish up here, Joey, I reckon I'd best go tell 'em at headquarters that they got a visitor on the grounds."

"You know where t' look for us later, Longarm." Joey nodded in the direction of the sutler's tent.

"I'll find you," Longarm promised. He stepped up onto a massive wheel so he could reach into the bed of the big freight wagon and retrieve his things from the floor of the driving box. He'd been hoping for a bath and a decent bed once they reached Brunot, but now he wasn't so sure what he could expect in the way of accommodations tonight.

Whatever the army chose to offer was what he would take. At most posts the regular way of such things was that a visiting deputy marshal was treated pretty much the same as a transient officer would be, the army for some reason having it in mind that a deputy was about on a level with a first lieutenant or perhaps a captain without a hell of a lot of time in grade.

Whatever they had to offer here, Longarm hoped it would include a good meal. Joey Dunfrey was no better a cook than Longarm was, and a proper supper served at a real table and with actual chairs to sit on would all be plenty welcome after the slow and bumpy ride down from Green River.

Longarm followed in the direction the corporal had gone just a few minutes earlier.

Chapter 9

"Get out!"

"Pardon me?"

"I said—"

"Oh, I reckon I heard you all right, Cap'n. But I got t' say that I never got a welcome like that'un at a army post, not ever before."

"Get out," the officer repeated. "I know what you are here for, and you have no jurisdiction. Now, get out of my sight and get off this military reservation before I have you clapped in irons, man."

Longarm blinked and pretended confusion. "No jurisdiction? Why, Cap'n, there's federal warrants out on that man. There surely are."

"Federal warrants? There can't be," the army officer countered. He was, in fact, a rather young-looking first lieutenant, despite Longarm's deliberate attempt to butter him up with a rank not yet earned. "It is strictly an army matter. No civilians have been involved."

"Cap'n, you sure got your information wrong 'bout that," Longarm drawled. "Why, the man held up a mail car, didn't he? Shot down a mail clerk, didn't he? Civilian mail clerk, I might add. *And* a government employee. If that don't give me jurisdiction, then I'd sure as hell like you t' tell me what does."

It was the army officer's turn to look confused. "Mail robbery? Bird Talks? I don't understand. I know of no mails being robbed."

"O' course it was mail robbery. Nothing t' do with no birds, though. Not 'less somebody was mailing a damn parrot in a cage or something. If they did, I never heard about it. No, sir,

40

I don't know what you mean there, somebody talking about birds involved. Just mail, that's all I know about. And o' course that shooting. Be my case anyway even without the shooting, but the mail clerk being killed, why, that makes it all the more important that we catch up with this sonofabitch."

"Catch up with—"

"Cap'n, do you happen t' have a hearing problem or what? What else would I be here for if not t' catch the S.O.B. and take 'im in?"

"But . . ." The officer shook his head. He was thoroughly confused now. Which Longarm intended but damn sure wouldn't have admitted to.

"Captain, I can assure you that I do have jurisdiction in this case. And I don't know how you could of heard anything different. What is it, does Bacon have friends around here that've been telling you about him? Well, no matter what they might've said, Cap'n, the man is wanted. And I'm here t' see that he's found."

"Bacon?"

"O' course. Who the hell else we been talking about?" Longarm retorted. "Clete Bacon. Cletus Anthony Bacon, if I remember the long version of it. Accused o' robbing the Ewe Ess mail on December . . . hell, I disremember the exact date now, a week, week and a half before Christmas it was, two years ago. That was over in Nebraska. Now we been tipped that Bacon's been spotted someplace around Vernal. Which is why I'm here right now."

"It is?"

"O' course it is. I come here t' requisition transportation from you, Cap'n. What the hell'd you think I come here about?"

The officer chose not to answer that. He puffed his cheeks and turned mildly red in the face and apologized several times but never did exactly respond to the question that had been put before him.

Longarm continued his outward pretense of innocent confusion. Inside he was about to bust from trying to keep himself from laughing at this poor lieutenant's befuddlement.

And of course Longarm hadn't really lied. Not precisely.

41

There really was—or more accurately, had been—a man known as Clete Bacon. Bacon really was wanted in connection with that train robbery and the mail clerk's death. And Billy Vail really had said there was a tip to the effect that Clete Bacon was spotted in the vicinity of Vernal, Utah. Never mind that everyone "knew" that Cletus Anthony Bacon had been murdered by the other members of his own gang after that Nebraska mail robbery. No body had ever been found when the other gang members were captured, tried, and sentenced. Nor any loot from the holdup, either. The gang members hadn't been inclined to talk much at the time. It was assumed that the money and the body were both buried in more or less the same place. Odds at this point were that neither would ever be found since the other members of the gang swung from a North Platte gallows more than a year back. There simply wasn't anyone left alive now who could bring an official close to the case by confirming Bacon's death.

An open and essentially unsolvable case wasn't generally the sort of thing a peace officer liked to have cluttering up his files. But they were stuck with this one, like it or not. It seemed only sensible to take advantage of it now.

"You say you wanted to requisition transportation?" the officer asked.

"That's right. Standard procedure, Cap'n. I'll want a horse to use while I'm here. Also billet and rations as necessary."

"You say this is standard procedure?"

"Cap'n, I don't mean t' pry an' sure wouldn't do nothing t' insult you, not for anything. But you did say you're the officer in charge o' Fort Brunot, didn't you?" Longarm managed to maintain a look of sympathetic concern.

"I . . . have recently found myself in command, yes. Our commanding officer, um, died. It's a long story. Nothing that should concern you, however."

"Yes, sir, whatever you say," Longarm said with a smoothly deceptive smile.

"And by the way, Marshal, our status here is only that of a camp, not a fort. It is Camp Brunot, you see. It remains to be seen if the post will be designated a fort at some time in the future."

"Thanks for straightening me out on that," Longarm told him solemnly. "I'll make sure I get it down right in whatever reports I write, Cap'n. Camp, not fort. Got it."

"And, um, I'm not a captain, Marshal. Only a lieutenant. First Lieutenant Henry Willis. In, uh, temporary command until Captain McGonegal returns from detached duty."

"I see."

"Perhaps you could, uh, join us in the officers' mess this evening?"

"That'd be nice, Cap'n. Oops, 'scuse me. Lieutenant." Longarm smiled and acted like he hardly knew one rank from the other anyhow, so what would it matter if the guy was a captain or a lieutenant or anything else.

"Seven o'clock, Marshal. I shall have the orderly show you to, um, visitors' quarters and point out the mess tent."

"That's real nice o' you, Cap'n. I mean, Lieutenant." Longarm touched the brim of his Stetson in a most unmilitary form of salute and smilingly bumbled his way out of the canvas-partitioned back end of the field tent where the post headquarters had been established.

It looked as if he was gonna get his cot and his meal after all. That had surely seemed to be in doubt for a while there.

Chapter 10

The Camp Brunot officers' mess was, predictably, another tent. A small one was all that was required. The collapsible trestle table was long enough to seat six diners . . . and was only half full once Longarm joined the gentlemen. The officer cadre of the post at the moment consisted of acting commanding officer First Lieutenant Henry Willis and, seated to Willis's right, Second Lieutenant Raphael deNunzio. Lieutenant deNunzio looked at least ten years older than Willis, but the difference in their rank required that the less-experienced officer be in charge here. Longarm was introduced to deNunzio and seated on Willis's left.

"Wine, Marshal?" deNunzio offered. "The menu tonight is leg of lamb with new potatoes and English peas, so I suggest a red. We have a nice burgundy, fruity and full-flavored, appropriately dry. Or a fair port if your taste runs more to the sweet beverages."

"I'm not that big on wine, Lieutenant."

"Oh?" The man tilted his head back a fraction of an inch and sniffed. "Pity." He looked away, obviously dismissing the visitor as being of no consequence.

Lieutenant deNunzio was something of a dandy, Longarm decided, with his curling mustache and longish dark hair. An effete poseur. Which might have had something to do with the discrepancies between his rank and his age. The sort of officer who would much prefer responding to a cello than a bugle. Longarm had to wonder what the fellow was doing out here on the fringes of nowhere when he would have been more at home in Washington or New York.

"No wine, Marshal?" Willis asked and, when the offer was again refused, clapped his hands. "You can serve now," he said in a slightly louder voice.

A slit in the back wall of the tent was pulled open, and a procession of Indian women came in bearing bowls and covered platters. The women were all young and reasonably attractive. There were four of them carrying the food plus another who held the canvas flap aside. Five young women, then, to serve two army officers. Not bad odds, Longarm conceded. For the white officers.

It occurred to him that these girls were the first Ute he'd seen since he arrived at Brunot. Even though the purpose of the post was to protect and to police the newly established Ute reservation here.

When all four serving girls were inside the mess tent, the fifth woman stepped in as well. She said something in her own tongue and pointed, and the other girls went into swift, practiced motion. Enameled domes were swept away to reveal the contents of the vessels. Portions were offered and demurely placed before the gentlemen, Willis being served first, then the guest, finally deNunzio. It was all done in silence and with great efficiency. If this had been a first-class restaurant, Longarm would have been impressed. As it was, he found the whole thing more puzzling than impressive. Did the army think the Ute were here to act as their damned servants?

"Thanks," he said to the girl who gently laid a slab of juicy lamb onto his plate. The girl blushed slightly and kept her eyes down. Not a single one of the girls made any eye contact with him, not even the one who seemed to be in charge. Longarm thought that young woman seemed vaguely familiar. He was sure he had never known her in the past, but he might well have seen her before.

The girls finished serving and withdrew as silently as they had come, leaving behind a meal that was superior to anything that could reasonably have been found anywhere between Denver and San Francisco.

Willis and deNunzio dug into their suppers without ceremony, and Longarm followed suit. The food tasted quite as good as the appearance and service implied that it should.

"We generally take our coffee after dinner," Willis ventured, "but you might like some with your meal, as you have no wine, Marshal."

"Whenever it's convenient."

45

Willis snapped his fingers. Immediately the tent flap was drawn back, and a Ute girl came in bearing a silver urn. She poured coffee for the guest and quietly withdrew.

"You boys don't have it bad here," Longarm said.

"Thank you." Willis smiled as if he'd been paid a compliment. Which was not at all the way the deputy had intended his remark.

But never mind that, Longarm conceded. There were areas where he might properly stick his nose and others where he didn't belong. This was one of those others.

"So tell me," Longarm said after the dishes had been cleared away and the cigars distributed. The two army officers and their visitor were leaning back with their ankles crossed and their bellies full.

"Yes?"

"I heard on the way down here that your commanding officer was murdered. Care t' tell me what happened?"

And just that quick the atmosphere inside the mess tent turned as cold as if a blue norther'd just whistled down off the snowcapped mountaintops.

Chapter 11

"This way." The sergeant major's voice was cold and uncompromising. He stood at the front tent flap like a saber blade come to life, just that rigid, seemingly that inflexible, too. He was looking at Longarm and pointing out into the night that had fallen while the officers were at their supper. The senior noncom had made his appearance within seconds after Longarm's not-really-casual question about the recent murders.

Nobody was gonna pass any secrets in the tents around here, Longarm silently observed. The Ute servants listened in at the back flap, waiting for a summons, and now there was this sergeant with an ear pressed to the canvas on the other end. Waiting for a different kind of summons? If there'd been one, Longarm hadn't noticed it. Regardless, it seemed like a guy couldn't fart around here without the whole camp knowing. That was something to keep in mind.

Longarm took his time about looking the sergeant over. Unlike the youngsters who constituted the officer cadre at Camp Brunot, this man had turned steely gray while in the service of his country. He had a sergeant major's stripes and rockers for chevrons and a stack of hashmarks on his sleeves that reached damned near from wrist to elbow. A man who'd worn the blue long enough to earn all those must've first enlisted when Hannibal was a shavetail. Likely he could have retired years ago but hadn't any home other than the army to retire to. Longarm had known men like that before, noncoms more often than commissioned officers. Frequently they were the people who were in real command, regardless of what the officially approved Table of Organization claimed.

"Were you speaking to me, Sergeant?" Longarm drawled without rising. He continued to sit at the trestle table with his legs crossed and a cigar clamped in the corner of his jaw.

"I was, indeed. Come this way. I'll show you to your quarters." He took a half step in the direction of the tent flap.

Longarm sat where he was, immobile except for a stream of pale smoke that trickled past his lips.

"I said—"

"Aren't you forgetting something? Sergeant?" Longarm's voice was every bit as cold as the noncom's was now.

The sergeant major didn't like that. His eyes narrowed, and the tendons at the sides of his neck corded and clenched. "You aren't no officer," he blurted. "I'm not required to 'sir' you."

Longarm feigned a yawn and turned to look at Lieutenant Willis, completely ignoring the sergeant now. "I believe you were about to tell me how your commanding officer was killed?"

Willis was busy sending nervous looks between his sergeant major and his dinner guest. It was clear that he didn't like this confrontation and equally clear that he wasn't sure what, if anything, he should do about it.

"Yes, well, um, actually, Marshal, I was thinking of turning in now. Uh, very heavy schedule tomorrow, you see."

"What, Willis? No brandy first? In a mess as civilized and pleasant as this one?"

"Our brandies aren't here yet, Marshal," deNunzio put in. "And you did say you don't care for wine."

"I suppose I can make do with the cigar and more coffee," Longarm said. He rolled the cigar in his fingers, turning it around and admiring the pale, clean ash.

"It is customary for guests—" the sergeant major began.

"What was his name?" Longarm asked of Willis, his voice calm and deliberate, too low to override the sergeant's but cutting through the noncom's words nonetheless.

"Who?" Willis responded, his eyes still darting back and forth between Longarm and the sergeant major.

"Your commander. A major, I believe I heard. Benson? Was that it, deNunzio?" Longarm acted as if the sergeant behind him simply did not exist. His attention moved from officer to officer. "Was the man's name Benson?"

"Benhurst," Willis corrected, acting as if the information came out in spits of careful resolve that he wouldn't say a word on that subject, because immediately afterward he seemed to go slightly pale and sent a worried look in the sergeant major's direction.

"Of course. Benhurst." Longarm nodded and drew on the cigar. It was a decent smoke. The officers of this outfit treated themselves mighty humanely even if they were stuck out here in the middle of nothing. "Stupid of me to've forgotten that, eh? You were going to tell me what happened to him?"

"Yes, but, uh . . ."

"We really do have to excuse ourselves, Marshal," deNunzio said. "Sergeant Major Gompert will take care of you."

"Gompert?"

"He is, um . . ."

"Is he that rude chap who doesn't know how to address an officer of the United States government?" Longarm wasn't generally one to give a fat crap about formalities or fanciness. But he could play the part of an asshole whenever it seemed necessary. And there was something about Sergeant Major Gompert that said he needed to have his ears pinned back right about now lest he think he could run a deputy United States marshal just like he ran this army post.

Willis looked utterly miserable. It was Lieutenant deNunzio who coughed delicately into his fist, then squared his shoulders and gave Gompert an order. "Sergeant Major, in future you will address Marshal Long with all due courtesy and respect. Is that clear, Sergeant Major?"

"Yes, sir. Perfectly clear, sir," Gompert snapped in a crisply military tone.

Longarm turned and looked at Gompert again. "Good evening, Sergeant Major. Pleasure t' meet you, I'm sure."

"My pleasure, sir." Gompert stood at rigid attention, his eyes fixed to the front and deliberately unfocused. The man's posture and bearing were correct enough to serve as a sculpted model of military perfection, suitable for the instruction of raw recruits for generations of soldiers to come.

"You wanted to say something to me, Sergeant Major?"

"I did, sir. If you would follow me, sir, it would be my pleasure to show you to our visiting officers' quarters. Sir."

49

"At your convenience, Sergeant Major," Longarm said pleasantly. He stood, stretched, said cheerful good-nights to Willis and deNunzio.

"This way, sir." Gompert's heels clacked loudly together, and he executed a snappy about-face. He marched the step and a half to the tent flap, returned to a posture of formal attention, and held the flap open for the "honored guest" to pass through.

Strange damned setup around here, Longarm thought as he ambled along at a deliberately slow and most unmilitary pace in the company of a man who seemed to detest him for no good reason whatsoever.

Except, Longarm amended, everyone has a reason for something like that. Always. The confusion only comes when somebody else doesn't understand what that reasoning is.

Chapter 12

Now, wasn't this almighty interesting, Longarm thought to himself as Sergeant Major Gompert showed him inside a spanking new wall tent and pointed out the few amenities such as water pitcher and basin, a thundermug, and a folding camp cot made up with woolen blankets but no sheets.

"The officers' sinks are over that way," Gompert said, pointing. He took down the lantern that was hanging from a nail tacked into the central tent pole and shook it to make sure it held a good supply of oil. "If you need anything else, sir . . ."

"If I do, Sergeant, I'll let you know."

"Yes, sir. I'm sure you will. Sir." Gompert snapped stiffly to attention and clicked his heels but quite properly refrained from saluting this man who was not an army officer. Very formal, very correct. Longarm nodded solemnly and told the man good night. "Good night, sir." Gompert wheeled and marched away into the darkness.

Longarm chuckled softly to himself and let the tent flap down over the entry, then dialed the lantern wick lower so that the flame became a faint glow, barely light enough to see by. And not enough to throw a hard silhouette against the thick canvas of the tenting material. There probably was no need for such a precaution here. But a man never knew.

Who, he wondered, did they think they were fooling? Did these blue-belly jerkoffs think a deputy U.S. marshal couldn't tell north from south once the sun went down? More likely they hadn't themselves bothered to think anything through, or they sure as hell would've done this different.

The point, of course, was that this tent, this brand-new visiting officers' quarters facility, hadn't been sitting on this spot just a few hours earlier when Longarm and the wagons rolled in.

Not that Longarm had bothered to memorize all the tents and structures that made up the partially built post, but the place where the wagons unloaded wasn't but a couple hundred yards away from where someone had hurried to put a bed for the unexpected visitor. It would have been impossible for him not to notice this isolated and obviously never-before-used tent if it had been in place then. The walls of this tent were new and starkly white, unlike the smudged and dingy shades of gray that softened the looks of a tent with time and repeated use.

They must not've thought about it was all Longarm could conclude. Or else they figured he was so dumb that he just wouldn't notice. Either way, they'd gone and made a mistake.

Likely there already was a tent set aside as quarters for visiting officers. Hell, there'd pretty much have to be one established for the benefit of the paymaster whose wagon and escorts traveled from one isolated post to another on an irregular schedule. It was not only regulation to have a VOQ, it was just plain sensible to provide well for the paymaster.

So why this charade now?

Longarm sat on the creaking, insubstantial edge of the folding cot and lighted a cheroot. He wished they'd thought to bring a decent chair in.

Why, dammit? There was a reason, of course. Just like there was a reason for Gompert's actions. A reason why no one here wanted to talk about the death of Major Benhurst. A reason why . . . Longarm sighed. There were lots and lots of reasons, dammit. He just didn't happen to know what any of them might be. Nor, in fact, what all the questions were that he needed answers for.

Why put him over on this side of the post by himself when a VOQ should already be available? That was a question he knew enough to ask.

The real VOQ was someplace where he wasn't welcome? Possible. Logical. Maybe even so. But at this point still only a guess.

He smiled thinly to himself. No reason why a man shouldn't go for a stroll in the evening air, was there? Nobody'd said anything to indicate he was to stay put. He stood and lifted the globe of the lantern so he could blow out the flame. With neither moon- nor starlight to soften the night, the interior of the tent was plunged into complete darkness. Longarm held himself still, wanting to wait a moment for his eyes to adjust before he set out.

A whisper of sound brought a chill to his spine, and he cupped the end of his cheroot inside a palm to hide the dull cherry glow of its coal lest the faint red light give him away. The sound, he was sure, was that of the tent flap being pulled back.

He blinked and strained to see. It was darker inside the tent than out. Dark enough inside that the charcoal of the night showed up as a pie-shaped gray wedge against the black of the tent walls.

The flap was pulled back only a few inches and then the faintly seen wedge of paler darkness was obstructed by a moving figure.

Someone was slipping inside the tent.

Longarm could hear breathing but no footsteps. He guessed the intruder was standing at the door waiting for his eyes to adjust, also.

Then what? Would he expect to find Longarm on the cot instead of standing by the center pole? Probably.

If he was an assassin, he was wanting to do his job in silence. Otherwise, it would have been quicker and safer to wait until he was sure the visitor was on the cot and then shoot through the canvas wall only inches away. There would have been no need for anyone to sneak inside like this.

But so soon after the lantern was extinguished? No one could believe Longarm would fall asleep that quickly after the light went out. So whoever this was surely knew him to be awake.

And therefore logically was *not* trying to knife him in his sleep.

Longarm relaxed and came upright, his knee joints popping. He raised the cigar to his mouth and drew on it, the brighter glow from the oxygen-enriched coal suddenly giving almost enough light to see by. Enough, anyway, that he could dimly see a shadowy presence at the front of the tent.

"Somethin' I can do for you t'night?" he drawled.

"Shhh!"

Longarm took another drag on his cheroot, again being rewarded with a hint of light. The figure seemed to be facing away from him now and peering outside between the folds of canvas that made up the doorway.

As if waiting to see if he was followed here?

Whatever this was about . . .

The intruder grunted and stepped away from the door, apparently satisfied.

"Now," Longarm said. "What is it brings you in here like this?"

The answer was a terse and staccato flow of words that Longarm couldn't begin to understand. There were only two things he could figure out from it.

One was that the language being spoken was Ute.

The other was that the person doing the talking was a woman.

Unless the officers and men of Camp Brunot had all of a sudden turned real generous toward visitors and sent this Indian girl as a cot warmer, maybe he was gonna get somewhere here after all.

Chapter 13

"I sure hope you c'n speak some English," he injected the first chance he got. Which wasn't all that soon. Whatever the girl was telling him, she had a lot to say.

"Shhh," she came back sharply.

"Fine," he said, this time in a whisper, "but I still don't speak no Ute."

"No Ute?"

"Thought I said that a'ready."

"But I am told you . . ." and then she was off in her own language again.

"Whatever that was," Longarm whispered at her, "you was told wrong, missy. I don't know a word you're sayin'." Which wasn't entirely true. A word slipped through now and then that sounded familiar, once in a while even one that he understood. But for damn sure he couldn't figure out the sense of what she was trying so hard to tell him.

"No Ute." This time it wasn't a question.

"Sorry."

"You are not . . . ?" and she said something in a singsong cadence that he knew he'd heard before but didn't know the meaning of.

"I am Long Arm."

"Long other thing, too?"

He laughed. There'd been a girl once. . . . "You know Swan, do you?"

She smiled. "Sister."

Which, Longarm knew, might mean anything from actual sister to distant cousin or even, by white reckoning, a totally unrelated stranger who nonetheless belonged to the same clan.

55

Indian kinships were a mystery that Longarm made no pretense of understanding. He was simply willing to accept at face value whatever was claimed and let it go at that.

"You are Long Long," the girl said. "I am Swimming Deer. You know my people. You come here to help."

"Yes." He thumbed a match aflame and lighted the lantern again, turning the wick down as low as it would go. The girl, young woman really, was the same girl who'd been supervising the table service earlier. She still looked vaguely familiar, but now he decided that was a resemblance to Swan. Maybe this girl really was close kin to the Ute girl Longarm had known before. "I want to help Bird Talks to the Moon. Do you know where I can find him?"

"Guardhouse," Swimming Deer said. "Big trouble, Bird Talks. Some say he shoot old major. Some say no."

"What does Bird Talks say?" Longarm sat on the edge of the cot and motioned for her to sit beside him so they could talk quietly and not worry about being overheard.

Swimming Deer shrugged. "His people don' be allowed to talk to him. Only soldier, and all soldier lie."

"No one has spoken with Bird Talks since he was arrested?"

"Not arrest. Detain," she corrected. Longarm wasn't sure just what the distinction was supposed to be between the two. Likely a matter of convenience, he decided. The army's convenience, that is. Never mind what the Ute did or did not find convenient, although he suspected that Bird Talks to the Moon was finding this whole affair to be mighty inconvenient.

"The point is, Swimming Deer, that nobody's talked to him."

"No one," she agreed.

"No one has tried?"

"No stone house for guard here, not yet. Dig big hole, put tent over. Soldier down in hole with Bird Talks. Gun, too. Watch him there. Listen. Any filthy Indian sneak close an' talk, guard would shoot. They say they shoot. We know they shoot. Same soldiers shoot before, Long Long. Too many Ute die then. Too many."

Longarm nodded. That was true, of course. It was part and parcel of the dustup that would go down in the history books as the Meeker Massacre. White men died in that genuine Indian uprising, and white women were raped. White soldiers came to put the uprising down, and a fair number of the soldiers died, too. History would carefully record the white deaths and the Indian perfidy that led to them. What history was likely to make light of if not ignore completely was that after the fighting started—never mind the why and the wherefore of the warriors who'd started the slaughter, Longarm didn't have to pass judgment on that subject and was glad he didn't—many more Ute than whites ended up bullet-riddled and broken. The soldiers who finished what those Ute warriors started hadn't achieved any gentle victory. So it was no wonder if the Ute now were wary of the men in blue. Because after all, it was the Ute who'd come off second best in that and virtually every other encounter with the blue-belly soldier boys.

Come to think of it, Longarm realized, the Ute tribe more than most had a history of getting the shit kicked out of them whenever they faced troops. The Ute nation had had some notable successes against white civilians. Not terribly long ago they'd virtually wiped out Pueblo, Colorado, in another less famous massacre. And, of course, they'd had their successes against white travelers and small parties of civilians moving through the mountains and along the rivers.

But in encounters with troops? He tried to call to mind one single occasion when the Ute won. Unlike with the Sioux, the Cheyenne, the Comanche, the Kiowa, or even the generally peaceful Navajo, with the Ute nation he couldn't think of any right offhand. Not one.

So maybe it was no great wonderment if this girl and her band got nervous about soldiers.

"I need to talk to him," Longarm said.

"Cannot do. Anyone come near, soldier shoot. They say so, Long Long. They shoot."

"I wonder . . ."

"Yes?"

He shook his head. He'd had a fleeting glimmer of an idea, but then it was gone too quickly for him to capture it. Something half-baked. Maybe it would come back. Or not.

"Your headman has protested to the army about this?"

"Oh, yes. Pissing Horse talk Lootnant Willis. Talk Lootnant Nunzie. Talk big Sergeant Gomber. They say Bird Talks is

57

soldier scout enrolled and legal. Now they detain but don'
arrest. No charge yet so no talk to him. That is why Pissing
Horse send for lady lawyer. She tell us she send for you. So we
wait for you. Now you come. Now you will fix everything."
Swimming Deer smiled. Longarm could tell that as far as she
was concerned, that explained it all right there. Hey, Long Arm
was here so everything was gonna be okay.

He only wished it was all that easy. But with no jurisdiction
he could claim and apparently no way to gather information
about the things that happened the day Benhurst and his escorts
died . . . shit, never mind making anything easy, Longarm'd
be happy if he just had reason to believe something would
be *possible* here. Rather gloomily he sighed and dropped the
butt of his cheroot onto the ground. In this game the army not
only held all the high cards, they weren't even letting him into
the play. And there didn't seem to be a damned thing he could
do about it.

Chapter 14

He'd thought she was ready to go, but she sat where she was, giving him a look that he could only interpret as being one of skepticism. Not that he blamed her. Hell, he was skeptical about his ability to help Bird Talks to the Moon, too.

"Is it true?" she asked.

"Kinda depends. Is what true?"

"What Swan tells me."

"I don't know what Swan told you, Swimming Deer."

She grinned. "Said you are long."

"I am Long. Custis Long. You know that."

"No no. Swan say you are long, Here." She said something in her own language and then added, "Long like horse is long." She reached over and quite matter-of-factly felt of his crotch. Longarm blinked. Swimming Deer only smiled. "Long," she affirmed. She allowed her hand to remain where it was, and Longarm's inevitable reaction to the warm pressure of her touch made her eyes go wide and her smile become even broader as the object in question thickened and began to extend against the restrictions imposed by the corduroy cloth of his trousers. Swimming Deer said something in her own tongue again, and this time she gently squeezed and stroked him.

"You'd best be careful what you get started," he warned.

Swimming Deer tossed her head to throw her hair behind her shoulders. She sat a little straighter beside him, her chest thrust forward and her head canted to one side. "You think I am pretty?"

"Very pretty," he agreed.

"Prettier than Swan?"

"Prettier than Swan." Which wasn't necessarily true. But

what the hell else was he supposed to say in a situation like this?

"Better fuck, too," Swimming Deer said firmly. And as if she was afraid he still might not get the point, she squeezed his cock again. Almost too hard for comfort, actually.

"I think you'd have to prove that to me," he told her.

Swimming Deer grinned. And began to shuck her clothes.

Swimming Deer's body was . . . adequate for the intended purposes. She was thick in the waist and thighs although otherwise slender enough. She had a dense, inky thatch of hair on her mound and breasts that were small and fluid, drooping toward her waist with their dark, raisinlike nipples pointed almost straight down. The color of her skin was a dusky, burnished copper. She wasn't going to win any prizes on the strength of sheer beauty.

On the other hand she was young. Her flesh was firm and the texture of her skin smooth and silky. As he discovered when she nuzzled close against him so he could stroke and pet and cuddle her.

The top of Swimming Deer's head came only throat high on Longarm. He could feel the heat of her breath on the bare skin of his chest while she fondled the length of his pulsing shaft. The Ute girl seemed to be impressed by the size of the particular tool she was admiring there. He almost expected her to whip out a seamstress's tape and measure him. She kept muttering things in her own language and now and then giggling. Every time she did that, she lightly squeezed his cock.

After several minutes of that, Swimming Deer smiled and sighed and with both hands pressed Longarm's rigid pecker tight against the skin of her belly. She nuzzled his chest and continued to hold his cock close against her with one hand while with the other she cupped and lifted his balls as if assessing their weight and their worth as companions to such a massive erection.

She whispered something he did not understand and then began to sway slowly to and fro. Her eyes sagged shut, and she chanted in a voice too soft for him to clearly hear.

Longarm placed his fingertips beneath her chin and tilted her head back, lifting her face so he could bend and place a kiss on her forehead. Swimming Deer seemed relatively unfamiliar with white ways and probably was not yet comfortable with the idea of kissing, which was a habit still new to her people.

There had been a time, a good many years ago now, when he hadn't understood that. Hell, kissing was kissing and everybody did it or anyhow wanted to from the first day a guy was old enough to get a hard-on, right? Not when Indians were concerned, he'd discovered that long-ago time.

The girl had been a Sac and probably should have known what was what, her tribe being no newcomers to contact with whites. Still, she'd been an innocent and protected young thing. But awfully pretty and near about as randy and lusty as young Custis—he was years away from being called Longarm then—once her blood and her skirt had both gotten lifted.

He'd crawled into the saddle and was happily pumping away, the both of them sweating and squealing and having a fine old time, until he decided to try that kind of kissing that he'd learned behind a good many barns and woodsheds back in West Virginia once upon a time.

When he stuck his tongue into the damn girl's mouth, she'd thought he was trying to strangle or maybe suffocate her or some such. The Sac girl had like to bit his tongue off that day and bucked him off her belly slicker than any horse he'd ever forked. She'd slapped the bejabbers out of him and gave him a cussing—least it'd sounded like a cussing; he'd never actually asked for a translation—and run off into the woods like a hare bolting for the briar patch.

The girl'd left Longarm—Custis, that is—sitting in a mess of dry leaves with an unspent wad in his cods and a look of deeply genuine puzzlement on his young face.

It was only later that he'd learned about the problem.

It'd been explained, actually, by the Sac girl's older sister, who was somewhat more familiar with white men and their peculiar—and to her mind disgusting—habits.

Lucky for Custis, though, the younger sister hadn't been able to complain to papa about the handsome traveler who'd tried to strangle her. She couldn't tell about that without telling on herself for taking that sashay into the woods. Otherwise, young Custis Long might've left his scalp in western Arkansas

61

and never have lived long enough to become a deputy U.S. marshal.

Lucky for him, too, the older sister had given him more than a simple explanation at the time. She'd also decided she wanted what the first girl ran away from, so young Custis was saved that day from having his balls swell up and burst and ruin him for life.

Ever since then, though, he'd understood that not all Indian girls wanted to have some hairy-faced white man spit into their mouths, which apparently was the way many still viewed the experience.

It was, Longarm had often thought, a damned peculiar reluctance on the part of girls who otherwise wouldn't think twice about eating a lightly roasted grasshopper or picking berries out of a pile of bear shit.

But everybody was entitled to their own preferences, he often said.

Now he settled for bussing Swimming Deer gently on the forehead and followed her down onto the ground when she sank to the hard earth—never mind the flimsy cot built wide enough for only one—and opened her thighs to him.

The Ute girl guided him onto her and kept on pulling, drawing him in as well as on.

She lifted her hips to accommodate his entry and gasped with pleasure when the length of him filled her.

He encountered a bit of resistance and figured that was all she could take, but Swimming Deer grabbed his ass with both hands and greedily hauled him deeper into her wet and ready depths. She wrapped her legs and arms tight around him and grunted with effort as she began to pump and throb beneath him.

Longarm figured he'd best get with the program or else be left behind, so he quit thinking about differences and commenced to paying attention to the similarities between this pleasantly eager girl and all the others he'd known.

Once he gave over to the things he was feeling and never mind pondering every-damn-thing, he found that Swimming Deer really was a better fuck than her sister/clansman/kin Swan. Or so Longarm was willing to believe until or unless Swan showed up to contest the title.

Chapter 15

"Begging your pardon, sir, but no one is allowed to pass without specific authorization. Sir." The soldier held himself at attention stiff as a ramrod with his Springfield rifle canted at a precise 45 degrees across his torso in a picture-perfect port-arms stance. His chin was tucked low and his eyes stared straight forward and slightly out of focus. He barked the warning crisply. There was about as much bend in this guy as there would have been in the barrel of his rifle. Maybe less.

Longarm drifted to a stop in front of the sentry, his own posture deliberately loose and easy. He was chewing a match stem—it had come in handy as a toothpick after breakfast, and he kept it dangling off his lip for the sake of appearances—and had his Stetson tilted onto the back of his head. If he looked like a harmless and halfway ignorant hayseed civilian, well, that would be just fine.

"Sure wouldn't wanta go where I ain't welcome," he drawled, adding a cheerful grin.

"Move along, please. Sir," the sentry barked.

"You bet, sonny." Longarm bobbed his head in complete agreement with the instruction. But remained standing right where he was. He was assuming that this tent had to be the guardhouse Swimming Deer had told him about last night, if only because it was the only one in sight that had an armed sentry posted before it. What he was hoping for was a word with Bird Talks to the Moon. A quick glimpse of the prisoner would have been enough for starters, though.

In order to buy a moment's time he fumbled in his coat pockets for a cheroot. Offered one to the sentry . . . an offer that was curtly refused, the young soldier's eyes still never actually focusing on anything. Held on to it while he needlessly picked his teeth for a moment and then flipped the match stem away. Dragged out a penknife and used it to trim the twist off the tail of his cheroot instead of biting it off the way he normally might. Anything to use up a little more time. "Sure you won't join me in a cee-gar, son?"

The sentry remained at rigid attention and didn't bother to answer.

Longarm lit up, smiled, exhaled with a loud sigh of contentment. "Now, that's a good smoke." He winked even though he wasn't at all sure the soldier could see it since the young man seemed to be functioning solely on peripheral vision here. "Pity I can't tempt you."

"Please move—"

"Yeah, yeah, I know. Movin' right along now, right." Even so, Longarm didn't start off. "You mind telling me where I went wrong, son? I set off looking for a Sergeant, um . . . fella in charge of the livestock detail, don't tell me, got his name on the tip o' my tongue practically, uh, Lieutenant Willis, he told me what it was not ten minutes ago, an' now it's slipped my mind . . . uh, Hanratty? Would that be it? Sergeant Hanratty?"

"You would be looking for Sergeant Hendricks, sir. I suggest you look for him along the picket line, sir. You won't find him here. Sir."

"Hendricks," Longarm mumbled. "Right. Hendricks. Thanks. You say there's a picket line, son?" He kept sneaking glances toward the wall tent behind the sentry. He already knew damned good and well where the picket line was. It was within rifle shot of the freight storage area and clearly visible from the visitors' quarters Longarm had been given last night.

"Sir, please. I must ask you to leave now." The soldier was commencing to sound annoyed.

"No need t' get riled here, sonny. I never meant to lose my way, y' know. Sure you won't change your mind about one o' these cigars? Mighty smooth smoke, these. I think you'd like 'em."

"Sir!"

Dammit, he did *not* want to turn and walk away right now. He kept seeing the canvas at the front of the tent shake and quiver even though there was no breeze at the moment. Somebody was moving around inside there. If he could delay just a bit longer . . .

"Right. I'm goin' now. Which way'd you say I should go t' find this Sergeant Hanratty?"

"Sergeant Hendricks, sir. And you can find him—"

"For God's sake, Abner, lighten up. Can't you see that the man is pulling your leg?"

The voice startled Longarm. It came from inside the tent. Which was not what was so amazing. The startling part was that it was a woman's voice. Guardhouse? Uh, apparently not. Not unless the way the army treated its prisoners had changed a whole lot since Longarm last heard.

"No, Abner, I suppose you can't see that at all, can you," the voice continued.

The soldier, Abner, blushed furiously but even then did not turn or allow his posture to slacken in the slightest. The young man turned so red that Longarm was fairly sure he could have lighted his cheroot by touching it to one of Abner's earlobes if the tobacco hadn't already been burning.

The tent flap behind Private Abner Whatever fluttered and was pulled open.

Abner continued to blush. Longarm quite frankly gaped.

"If the army has started issuing one of you for every post, ma'am, please point the way t' where I can go enlist." Longarm swept his Stetson off and made a leg in the lady's direction.

"How gallant of you, Marshal." There was no false modesty in the woman. She looked him in the eye and turned her shoulders half away so he could get an even better look.

And there was plenty there to look at, plenty worth the looking.

The lady was tall and statuesque. Her waist was tiny and her bosom imposing. She wore her hair swept high in a cascade of tight blond curls that left an unusually long and patrician neck exposed. A cameo and ribbon tied tight at the throat emphasized her neck. Her cheekbones were high and slightly prominent. Her mouth and cheeks were rosy, practically aglow with healthy vitality. Unless, that is, she used artificial means to achieve the coloring. If she did, she did it damned well. From a distance of eight or ten paces Longarm couldn't tell.

The overall effect was that of a lady, the genuine article all patrician and elegant and poised.

"Simple honesty from a simple man, ma'am, without the grace for gallantry. But you have the advantage of me as you already know who I am."

"Please, ma'am," the sentry pleaded. "You shouldn't be doing this."

"Have I been confined to my quarters, Abner? Without anyone bothering to inform me? How rude."

"You know you haven't, ma'am. But—"

"I know what your orders are, Abner, but really. It isn't like a United States marshal would offer me any harm."

"No, ma'am, but—"

"Don't argue, Abner. It doesn't become you."

"No, ma'am." The young sentry looked quite thoroughly miserable now.

The woman smiled and motioned Longarm forward, holding her hand for him to kiss.

"Ma'am," he said.

"I am Clytemnestra Benhurst, widow of Major Donald Benhurst. And you, I am told, are Custis Long."

"A pleasure to meet you, Mrs. Benhurst."

"The pleasure is all mine, Marshal." She gave him a looking-over that was so frank an appraisal that Longarm was glad sentry Abner was facing in another direction. Mrs. Benhurst's attention seemed to be locked just a little ways below Longarm's belt buckle for most of the time she was inspecting him. Surely she couldn't have been told anything about . . . no, not possible, it was only coincidence and a widow's appetites.

"Thank you, ma'am."

"Ma'am?" she mocked, her eyelashes fluttering with outrageous coquetry. "Am I so ancient, sir, that I must be called ma'am?"

It was probably the game she hungered for here, Longarm guessed. Not a man really but the pleasures of flirtatious dalliance. On a large post there would be officers and ladies aplenty to provide Mrs. Benhurst with amusement. Here there was damn-all for a social life. And with her husband dead . . .

Come to think of it, why would she be staying here with her husband murdered? Then he realized there could be a score of answers to that one, including a simple desire to see her husband's supposed killer brought to justice. If so then the lady and Longarm had something in common.

Longarm smiled and offered the customary protestations in response to the lady's blatantly leading comment. No, she was anything but ancient. She was, in fact, an oasis of beauty in the midst of desert.

Mrs. Benhurst simpered. She preened. She damned near commenced to purr with satisfaction when the tall and handsome deputy assured her she was the prettiest thing between New York and San Francisco.

Longarm laid the butter on with a trowel. Hell, why not? Didn't cost anything and made the widow woman feel better about herself. The only thing he minded about it was that poor Abner was having to stand there at attention an' listen to it.

"It is *so* nice to entertain a *gentleman* again, Marshal." She didn't mention Willis or deNunzio by name. But then she didn't have to under the circumstances, did she?

"My pleasure, Mrs. Benhurst."

"Oh, that sounds so formal. And I do sense that we shall become great friends, don't you?"

"I would count it an honor to be named among your friends, Mrs. Benhurst." He bowed again.

"Then you must call me Sly and I shall call you Custis."

"Sly?"

"Clytemnestra, which my nanny shortened to Cly and my brothers, the rascals, changed to Sly. I've borne it as a pet name so long, I scarcely remember that it carries other connotations."

"Sly it shall be," Longarm promised.

"Abner, run tell Cook that I shall have a guest for dinner this evening. My newest dear friend Custis will be joining me."

"Ma'am, you know I can't—"

"Oh, pooh, Abner. You take everything much too seriously, do you know that? All right, though, you may wait until you are relieved here. Then deliver my message to Cook, if you please."

"Yes, ma'am, I'll do that, ma'am." Abner completed the entire conversation without once ever relaxing his posture or turning to look in the direction of Longarm and the lady.

Sly Benhurst winked at Longarm and laid her fingertips delicately on his forearm. "Now, if you would be so good as to accompany me, dear Custis, I normally take a constitutional at this hour."

"A what-which?"

She laughed. "A walk, dear. A stroll. It tones and supples the limbs, dear, and encourages regularity of the bowels. I take one every morning at this time. And although I know I could rely on your good offices for my protection, dear Abner there will no doubt insist on following his orders to the letter and trudging along behind." She turned to send a glare in the direction of the back of Abner's neck. "*Not* close enough to eavesdrop, however."

Abner didn't say anything, but he heard, all right. The nape of his neck turned bright red beneath his infantryman's kepi.

"At your service, m—" Longarm grinned and quickly corrected himself. "Sly." The three of them set out, Longarm with the lady on his elbow ambling along in the morning sunshine and Private Abner marching stiffly behind them at a distance of fifty paces or so.

Chapter 16

Sly Benhurst herself raised the subject that had made Longarm eager to accompany her on her morning constitutional. She directed their travel out of the camp and off toward the north, away from the streambed that at this time of year was bone dry but where the Camp Brunot wells had been dug. Just as they were about to get out of sight from the tents that made up the growing post, she pointed to the top of another white-wall tent, the roofline of which could barely be seen beyond a low ridgeline.

"That is the guardhouse," she said. "That is where they are holding the man who murdered my dear Donald."

"Oh?" Hell, he would have had an awful time trying to find the guardhouse with it stuck way out here. Longarm was grateful to Mrs. Benhurst for showing it to him. "I don't mean to bring up unpleasant memories, Sly, but naturally I've heard something about your husband's, um, death. You said he was murdered?"

"Yes."

"I understood he was fighting Indians at the time?"

"My husband did not die in battle, Custis. Donald was the kind of man—the kind of officer—who would have been proud to die for his regiment. But he hadn't that privilege, you see. His death was, as I said, a murder. A sordid thing, really, with neither honor nor glory attached. We were en route here from our previous posting. There were four of us in the wagon, you see. An ambulance. It had been sent to collect us and carry us to our new quarters. I daresay we would have been all right had we waited and come along with the freight wagons. There was a train of them driving a day or so behind, bringing the materials that came on the same train Donald and I rode out.

We could have gone with those wagons. But Donald was eager to rejoin the regiment. We had taken a leave, you understand, and he had been on detached duty before that. At Headquarters for the Department of the Missouri in St. Louis. Donald was assigned there for the past several years." There was a quality in her voice that sounded wistful and homesick when she said that. But no wonder. Sly Benhurst was the sort of lady who would be in her element at a major headquarters posting like that, particularly one in so civilized an environment as St. Louis.

"Your husband wasn't with the regiment then, when, uh . . ."

"The massacre at White River? I'm a big girl now, Custis. You don't have to tiptoe around that. I am fully aware of the atrocities the Ute committed there."

"Sorry."

"To answer your question, no, he was not. We were in St. Louis at the time. Donald hadn't actually been posted with his regiment for some years now. He was terribly eager to rejoin it. And that is why he wasn't willing to travel at the slow pace of those freight wagons. He wanted to rush ahead. Couldn't wait that one day more it would have taken to come in company with the teamsters." She sighed. "I daresay Donald and those poor men still would have been alive today if we had waited."

"I still don't understand what happened that day. Pardon my curiosity, please, Sly, but I frankly would have expected a hue and cry about another Ute uprising. Instead, well, the army has been most reluctant to even mention the deaths."

"That has been my fault, I fear. Or at any rate, for my benefit."

"I'm afraid I don't understand."

"We are going to be wonderfully good friends, Custis. I do sense this. So I hope you will permit me to be perfectly honest with you."

"Please do."

"As I said, dear, I was in that ambulance with Donald and the two privates who were our escort. The privates . . . I'm afraid I don't recall their names now; isn't that perfectly horrid of me? . . . anyway, they were riding on the driving seat, and

70

Donald and I were in the ambulance with the side curtains rolled down against the dust. The choice was between being miserable from heat, you see, or choking in dust. Donald had the side curtains closed at my request. If they hadn't been . . ." She paused, then shrugged.

"The ambulance stopped, and Donald went forward to ask the driver why. I could hear the conversation, of course. There was a scout approaching on the road. An Indian. The enlisted escorts said they knew the man, so there was nothing to worry about. Donald said that was all right, then. The men asked permission for a rest break since we happened to be halted. Donald agreed. The driver set the brake, and the other soldier came around to open the door for me. Donald handed me out to him. I . . . just as I was stepping out of the ambulance, the Indian scout reached the ambulance. He stopped and . . . stared. I suppose my presence took him by surprise, and he had no chance to prepare himself for being around a white woman. I didn't think much of it at the time, you see. But he stared. He seemed . . . smitten, if I may be so bold as to say it."

"Your beauty is enough to command that reaction in any man, m—Sly."

She smiled. "How nice of you to say so, dear. Thank you."

"You were saying?"

"Yes, of course. This Indian scout, who the escorts vouched for, stared for a bit. Then he got off his horse and stared some more. I was becoming quite uncomfortable and wouldn't have wanted to be left alone with him. I felt . . . oh, my, in retrospect—" she sighed again—"I felt a certain amount of relief when the Indian walked along behind when Donald and the two soldiers went off away from the ambulance to relieve themselves. Which they couldn't do close by, of course, as I was there. They walked away from the wagon somewhere.

"The next thing I knew, I heard gunshots. Several of them, one very quick after another. I don't recall how many exactly, only that they came very close together. I thought . . . a snake, perhaps, something like that. I know only that I wasn't particularly alarmed. After all, an army wife hears gunfire often. But it is only for practice or as a salute. I'd never heard gunfire before that was . . . deadly in intent."

"No, of course not." Hardly unusual, Longarm realized. Most people pass their lives without ever having to fear loud noises. Even army wives.

"A minute later. Less. I heard footsteps. It was the Indian. I thought . . . I don't know what I thought, exactly. I still wasn't frightened. The Indian approached me. He . . . took me by the arm. I tried to pull away. He wouldn't let go. He dragged me to his horse and . . . put me up on it. In front of him. He . . . held on to me. Spurred the horse and took me away. I never . . . saw Donald again. Not alive, that is. The Indian knew a place. It was only a few miles distant from where he'd waylaid Donald and the soldiers. He took me there. I don't know what he intended to do with me. Beyond . . . the obvious, that is. I mean to say that I don't know what his long-term plans were. Or even if he had any. I suppose the whole thing was a spontaneous matter. Spur of the moment and all that. Probably he never thought it through. He saw me and wanted me and the white men had their backs turned. So he acted. It was . . . the next day before help arrived. More than twenty-four hours later. If you don't mind, dear Custis, even though I know we will be wonderful friends, if you don't mind, dear, I should like to speak no more about what happened during that period of time."

"Of course not," he agreed quickly. He could see that her eyes were moist and sparkling, welling full with tears she was struggling to keep from spilling.

"So you see, dear Custis, the reason the regiment is making no public issue of this is out of regard for my feelings. If the Indian was charged, brought to trial, and hanged . . . I should have to testify, you see. The . . . indignities he imposed upon me would have to be discussed in an open court. They would become public record. Everyone would know . . . would in their mind's eye see each of those horrid things happening all over again. All the details. Every man who looked at me . . . ever again . . . he would know. I . . . couldn't bear that, Custis. It is bad enough that people must whisper in speculation. If they knew the awful truth . . . the details . . ." She shuddered, and now the tears did begin to flow.

It was all Longarm could do to keep from wrapping a protective arm around her shoulders and holding this poor, abused woman close to him.

It was damned near all he could do to keep from walking over to that guardhouse tent and blowing a hole through the head of the sonofabitch Bird Talks to the Moon, who'd done such a thing to this dear and innocent lady. Blow the bastard's head clean off his shoulders and then reload and shoot into the dead body some more.

Anyone who would go and do something like Bird Talks to the Moon did . . .

Longarm cleared his throat. Maybe he couldn't offer much in the way of comfort to this poor, sad woman. But he could let her know that he cared, dammit.

He reached over and gently, gently patted the small, soft hand that lay trustingly on his forearm as they walked. "If there is anything I can do, Sly. Ever. Anything at all. You just let me know, hear? And I mean that. Anything whatsoever. You just name it, an' I'll dang sure do it."

"Thank you, Custis." The widow Benhurst dabbed a hankie at her tearing eyes and managed a weak smile. "I shall treasure your offer always, dear. Thank you."

Longarm felt a swelling in his neck and shoulders, as if he were preparing himself for combat, and the look he sent in the direction of the guardhouse tent was murderous.

Chapter 17

They hadn't gone another hundred yards before the morning constitutional was interrupted. A soldier wearing blues and carrying a Springfield with bayonet attached came loping after them.

"Don't pay him any mind," the widow Benhurst said. "Jason is here to relieve Abner."

The soldier, however, only slowed to say something to Abner, then jogged on toward Longarm and Mrs. Benhurst while Abner turned back toward the post.

"I think he wants to tell you something, Sly."

"This is all such a bother. As if now was when I needed protection. Where were they when . . ." She sighed and gave her head an impatient toss. "Forgive me. I shouldn't say things like that. I really *must* remember to be good in the future, mustn't I?" However reluctantly, though, she did stop and wait for the panting, sweating young private to catch up. It was a warm morning, and Longarm knew how hot the army's woolen blues were. The boy no doubt would have been more comfortable wearing light canvas fatigues, but the obligation to guard the dead commander's widow was much too formal and ritualized for that.

"Good morning, Jason."

The private blushed so quickly that Longarm suspected Jason was more than half in love with his pretty charge. The other half of that emotion was probably awe. To a youngster like Jason a beautiful lady, an officer's lady at that, would be as remote and unattainable as an angel.

"M-m-ma'am," he sputtered, coming to a position of attention and executing a well-intentioned but rather sloppy rifle salute. "Begging your pardon, ma'am, but I'm to tell the marshal that he's wanted in camp, ma'am."

"Must you, Jason? Mr. Long and I have been having such a nice talk this morning."

"I'm sorry, ma'am, but I got to."

"Very well, then," she said with a pout.

Jason saluted the lady again and turned his attention to Longarm. "Sir. You are directed to report to Lieutenant deNunzio. Immediately, if you please. Sir."

"Thank you, Jason."

The boy acted as if he hadn't heard. Hell, probably he hadn't. His eyes were fixed worshipfully on Mrs. Clytemnestra Benhurst, and likely Jason wasn't aware of anything or anybody else in the whole universe right at that particular moment.

"If you will excuse me, Sly?"

"If I must."

Longarm removed his Stetson and bowed as elegantly as he knew how.

"Remember, Custis. Dinner tonight. You promised."

He hadn't, actually. But he wasn't going to correct such a picayune detail as that.

"Would eight be convenient?" she asked.

"Your convenience, madam, is my command."

"La, sir. Now I'm not so sure I am willing to release you to Lieutenant deNunzio." She laughed and turned away, touching young Jason on the wrist and bringing another flush of bright scarlet to the boy's ears. "You will watch for snakes, won't you please, Jason? You know how frightened of them I am," she was saying as she continued her constitutional.

Longarm turned and headed back toward Camp Brunot without any particular haste. Whatever deNunzio wanted wasn't likely to be anything worth working up a sweat over.

"Frankly, sir, if I had my way about it, I would ask you to remove yourself from this post. Civilians have no place on a military reservation." DeNunzio sniffed and twisted one heavily waxed mustache end. It already looked sharp enough to be dangerous.

"Doing my job, Lieutenant. Just like you're doing yours. And I believe if you look in the book of regs, where it says something about employees o' the federal government and the assistance t' be offered—"

"I am familiar with the regulations, thank you," deNunzio said with frosty disdain.

Longarm gave the fella a look of mild amusement. "Point is, Raphael, so am I."

DeNunzio sniffed again.

Longarm crossed his legs and busied himself with the chore of getting a cheroot lighted. If the lieutenant wasn't in any hurry now that Longarm was here . . .

"I have been instructed to inform you, Marshal, that the Ute Indian known as Pissing Horse requests to speak with you. I repeat, sir, it is against my better judgment to allow you to—"

"Ease off, Raphael. I think I know what bee is buzzin' around in your bonnet, an' you don't hafta be so edgy about it. All I come here t' do is look for a civilian criminal name of Cletus Bacon." And if that wasn't entirely true, well, there was no point in going into it with deNunzio now.

"But—"

"You gonna let me finish this, Raphael?"

DeNunzio glowered but this time kept his mouth shut.

"In case you wanta know, mister, me and ol' Pissing Horse go back a ways. He knows me from before. An' I know him. The old bastard's a thief an' a liar an' no doubt a murderer, too. But him and me have got drunk together and laughed together and if I didn't say howdy to him now that I know he's in the neighborhood, it'd be an insult o' the worst kind. And I'm sure you don't wanta be the cause of any more uneasiness between the Ute nation an' the one you and me both serve. So whyn't you just back away an' let your water come down off the boil."

"I didn't know—"

"You didn't know a lot o' things an' still don't, Raphael."

"I assumed—"

"Helluva bad thing t' do sometimes, this assuming stuff. Gets a guy in trouble more often than not."

"My interest is in preserving the honor of this regiment, sir. I meant no—"

Longarm interrupted him again, this time wordlessly. The tall deputy had turned steely cold. He leaned forward and fixed deNunzio with an accusing glare. "My interest, mister, is in preserving the honor an' the integrity o' this country. I suggest, sir, that yours oughta be the same."

"I didn't mean—"

Longarm stood. "Where is Pissing Horse?"

"But I didn't—"

"Fine. I'll find 'im myself." Longarm whirled around and stalked out of the tent that served Camp Brunot as the adjutant's office.

Chapter 18

Hendricks, the sergeant in charge of livestock and transportation at Brunot, turned out to be a gray-haired lifer who appreciated the small perks that his position entitled him to. "Very nice cigar, sir," he said approvingly as he drew on the cheroot Longarm had just lighted for him.

"What these cigars need, Sergeant, is the mellowing influence of a good whiskey. Seems a pity it's so early in the morning."

"So it is, sir, a great pity, indeed." Hendricks grunted and puffed on the smoke a second time.

"There is a post trader's tent, I would assume, where a man can buy a libation?" Longarm asked.

Hendricks smiled. "Right over there. Would you be seeing the roof of it, sir?"

"I believe I do."

"No whiskey service at this hour, o' course," the sergeant said.

"And a very sensible rule that is, too," Longarm agreed.

"The gennulman as runs the place commences service promptly at the sounding o' retreat," Hendricks observed.

"Now, that is a fine thing to know, Sergeant. Is it possible that I might run into you there?"

"Possible, yes."

"And if I happened to . . . sometime tonight, say . . . we might want to test my claim that these smokes taste best with a dram on the tongue, mmm?" It had occurred to Longarm that he'd promised those teamsters a drink, too, and hadn't yet paid up. Tonight he ought to be able to take care of them and Hendricks, too. He would have to remember to pass the word to them later.

"We might could," the sergeant said. "If we bumped into each other there." He winked and sucked on the cheroot. "By accident, like."

Longarm grinned and nodded. He and Hendricks understood each other.

The problem—solved now so that no problem existed at this point—was that there seemed to be only one saddle horse on the entire Camp Brunot compound. There were mules. There were oxen. There were a handful of heavy-bodied draft cobs. But only one horse fit for use under saddle. Longarm had no idea if the animal belonged to Willis or to deNunzio. Furthermore, he had no intention of asking.

"Would you care to be using your own saddle now, sir, or shall I provide one?"

"This one will be fine, thanks."

Hendricks insisted on taking the McClellan from Longarm and saddling the horse for him.

"Thank you, Sergeant, you're very kind."

"Only going by the book, sir. Strictly by the book is what it is, sir." The old boy winked again and gave Longarm a snappy salute as the deputy cantered out in the direction of the Ute camp.

The Ute village had been established, so he'd been told, some seven miles west of the army post. The terrain changed dramatically in that short distance. Camp Brunot was sited on arid, near-desert soil, yet to the west the country became progressively greener and more gentle as it rose toward a string of low mountains that no doubt captured and spilled the prevailing rains and winter snows. The closer to the mountains the wetter, and for some reason the army had chosen to locate on some of the poorest ground around.

The soldiers Longarm talked to assured him it would be difficult even for a pilgrim to lose his way between Brunot and the village. There was a wagon road leading from one to the other, used by wagons delivering rations to the Ute and used as well, Longarm discovered for himself, by army teamsters who were hauling building stone and timber back to the new fort.

He would have thought there was stone enough aplenty for building purposes there at the camp. Then, when he saw what the wagons were hauling, he understood. Close to the post there was only ordinary rock. Somewhere still ahead the soldiers were quarrying shale that broke into flat, easily fitted slabs that would be ideal for the sort of construction the army wanted, especially if the soldiers who were doing the work were not particularly skilled as masons.

The timber, he guessed, would be reserved for ridgepoles and roof poles and probably would be covered with dirt and sod. Or even thin splits of shingle shale if that degree of permanence was desired.

About five miles from Brunot the road forked, one branch leading north into a shallow canyon and the other continuing along the dry creek bed the road had paralleled all the way from the fort.

No one had mentioned the fork, dammit. Probably because to them it was so obvious. Longarm wanted the road, not the quarry path. Never mind that to someone not familiar with them the two sets of ruts looked exactly the same.

Longarm sat on the leggy thoroughbred that he'd been loaned and pondered which road he should take.

Then he smiled. A mile or so up the creek bed he could see the slow, crawling approach of a freight wagon. Coming from the quarry, no doubt. Therefore, it was logical to assume that the other fork, the one leading into the canyon, was the one that would take him to Pissing Horse's village.

Of course, he might have waited for the wagon to reach the fork so he could ask. Or he might have spurred his horse ahead to meet the wagon and inquire.

Either of those, though, would be time-consuming.

The hell with it.

He reined the horse away from the creek bed and bumped it into a slow jog, quickly leaving the fork and the wagon traffic behind.

The path meandered into the wide, shallow canyon bottom and was quickly lost to all view from outside the canyon.

So gradually the changes almost weren't noticeable, the sides of the canyon steepened until they became abrupt, indeed. So sharp, in fact, that it would no longer be possible for a man on horseback to climb out to either side. A man afoot would be able to scramble up or down, but anyone on a horse would be able to proceed only forward or back.

Towering over the road to either side at the top of the canyon walls now were outcroppings of bare rock squared off so sharply they looked like medieval battlements and castle walls.

Anyone posted atop those walls would have complete command over . . . Longarm scowled and told himself his mind was playing damnfool tricks with him. Pissing Horse was an old friend. And the Ute nation wasn't at war with anybody now.

And a damned good thing, too, he thought as he tipped his head back and looked at the tall, forbidding walls he was riding between.

The two sides of the canyon were pinching closer together. Now there wasn't anywhere on the floor that a man could get out of rifle range if somebody on either side wanted to lay down a field of fire.

Not that anybody would, of course.

But . . .

He reached for a cheroot and lighted it, trying to ignore the way the back of his neck felt tight and creepy-crawly as if a passel of bedbugs had begun marching back and forth under his collar.

There was no reason to be jumpy now, he kept telling himself. No reason at all.

He blew his match out and flicked the spent stem away. Feeling like an idiot but unable to keep himself from doing it, he stood in his stirrups and begun an intense visual search of the rimrock and the canyon walls.

Longarm found himself wishing he knew this borrowed horse better, wishing he knew if he could trust it for a warning, a flick of the ears or perhaps a snort or nicker if there was danger about.

He touched the grips of his Colt, reached down to touch as well the butt of the Winchester in its scabbard, both movements a purely involuntary need for the reassurance of knowing the weapons were where they should be.

He rubbed the palm of his right hand against the corduroy cloth that covered his thigh. His hand was already dry. But still . . .

Behind him he heard a crash of falling rock, and he jerked in his saddle, either the noise or its rider's movement startling the horse into a jumpy plunge.

Longarm clamped his knees tight on the horse's barrel and concentrated on stopping the impending runaway. He kept a firm hand on the reins without yanking on the bit and crooned softly to the animal. He could feel it tremble beneath him, but after a moment the tension went out of it and he could let the reins go slack once more.

When he looked up again, he was surrounded by a score or more of wildly painted Indian warriors.

Longarm's eyes went wide.

And the Indians began to screech and whoop and brandish weapons as they leapt and howled and raced down the canyon walls on both sides of him.

"Aw, shit," Longarm muttered.

Chapter 19

Longarm kept his hands away from his guns. That was one of the most difficult things he'd ever gone and done, but he managed it.

The thing was, in spite of all the noise and carrying on, nobody was shooting. Yet. He'd be as happy if nobody ever got around to it since he was outnumbered by something on the order of twenty to one.

The borrowed horse was getting more and more nervous, and Longarm had to concentrate on keeping the animal from bolting for safety. An attempt to run out of the circle, even one that Longarm had no control over, might start the gunfire. If he stayed right where he was, though . . .

While the yammering warriors closed in on him, he was trying to figure out just who in the hell they were.

They didn't look like any tribe he recognized, actually.

Their war paint was more drab than gaudy. Brown and gray and some dull ochre. None of the bold and vibrant hues one would normally associate with war paint.

And their clothes. Shit, these guys were dressed like . . . well, pretty much like a bunch of gatepost idlers who'd gone and taken their shirts off. He could see more shoes than moccasins. Blue jeans and army woolens chopped into short pants. But no breechclouts. No headbands. Certainly no dress-up feather bonnets or any of that fancy foofaraw.

This was about the craziest damned war party he'd ever come across.

Not that that mattered. There were enough of them that they didn't have to follow the rules of normal behavior to get their point across. Whatever it turned out to be.

Longarm took a deep breath and did his level best to pretend that none of this was bothering him the least little bit.

While the crazy sonsofbitches were closing in around him, in fact, he fished around in his coat pocket and found a cheroot to gnaw on. He didn't try and light it yet, though. It wouldn't have done to let it show if his hand went to shaking.

"Ho ho ho, Arm Long. Ho, ho."

Longarm looked up the slope.

And grinned.

"Pissing Horse, you bastard!"

"Pissing Horse make you piss your pant, Arm Long?"

"You know better, you ol' sonofabitch."

Pissing Horse laughed and hobbled slowly down the slope behind the rest of the Ute men.

Now that things were slowing down some, Longarm could get a good look at this "war party."

No wonder they'd looked so odd. The so-called war paint wasn't anything more than dirt and rock dust rubbed onto their faces.

And, hell, they *were* just a bunch of guys who'd taken their shirts off so they could scare the shit out of somebody by playacting as a war party.

"You ol' sonofabitch," Longarm repeated with a grin as Pissing Horse reached the bottom of the canyon and came over to Longarm's side.

The two shook hands. Pissing Horse looked inordinately pleased with himself for having gotten the better of Longarm with his joke.

"Is a good day to die, Arm Long?" the old man asked.

"Not the one I'd pick on my own," Longarm admitted. "But no worse 'n any other, neither." He smiled and gave Pissing Horse a cheroot, then leaned down to light it for him before firing up his own. No tremble in the hands now. "What are you doing down here trying t' frighten innocent travelers, Pissing Horse?"

"Innocent? Where?" Pissing Horse made a big show of looking around in search of somebody innocent. Longarm saw that most of his warriors could understand some English, too, because most of them enjoyed that exchange.

"You know what I mean."

"Come out to meet Arm Long, we," Pissing Horse said

solemnly. "Know our friend come from fort. Come meet him, yes? Then see Arm Long has become dumb fuck since knew him last, eh? Arm Long take wrong fork. This road" —he said something in his own language— "no good. Don' go to village, eh? Go where blueleg sojer dig rock. So" —Pissing Horse grinned, exposing yellow stumps where teeth used to be—"we take short way. Up high, eh?" He pointed toward the west rim above them. "Get ahead. Think it good joke to scare Arm Long. Make him piss pant. Let me see, Arm Long. Let me see your pant."

Longarm chuckled and stood in his stirrups, displaying a dry crotch for all to inspect. He thought Pissing Horse looked disappointed.

"Good joke anyway, yes?"

"Yes, it was," Longarm agreed. "Damn you."

That tickled Pissing Horse and got him and the rest of the Ute welcome party/war party to laughing all over again.

"Come, Arm Long. We eat, get drunk, let you screw my youngest wife."

"Dammit, Pissing Horse, your youngest wife is older'n my grandmother."

"You gonna insult me by refusing my wife, Arm Long?"

"Damn right I am, Pissing Horse. If you want her pleased, you gotta do it yourself."

The old bastard threw his head back and roared. "See?" he pointed out to the other Indians. "Arm Long not so dumb after all." He motioned for the others to head back up the steep canyon wall to where they'd left their horses. Pissing Horse himself, though, had no intention of climbing up that wall at his age. Longarm had no way to know just how old that was, but he would have guessed it somewhere in the man's eighties. And maybe more. For a man of those years, coming down a wall that steep was one thing, going up quite another. Instead, Pissing Horse held a hand up to Longarm for a boost and helped himself to a seat behind Longarm's cantle.

It was, Longarm reflected, a rather good thing that the horse didn't balk at being ridden double. It would've been a helluva note if he was responsible for the old Ute headman getting thrown and maybe killed.

"Slow, Arm Long, slow now, eh? Older I get, the skinnier

my ass get. No meat no more. So go slow, Arm Long. Don'
bump now."

Longarm chuckled aloud and put the horse into a bone-
jarring trot.

But only for a few paces, just long enough to raise a shriek
of discomfort from the old Indian. Then he brought the horse
back to a gentle walk. Longarm didn't figure that made him
even with Pissing Horse yet, but it was better than nothing.

"Damn, Arm Long. You a mean sum'bish," Pissing Horse
complained, rubbing at his scrawny backside and grinning.

Longarm laughed and held the horse to the slow and easy
gait.

Chapter 20

The Ute village was farther along in its construction than Camp Brunot.

For that matter, Longarm thought, it might end up being the more modern and attractive community as well.

The army was making do with native stone and locally cut rough timber for their building materials. Here lumber had been hauled in, no doubt at considerable expense, and was being used to erect small houses. The few that were finished had been painted white, and several even had low picket fences encircling them.

Longarm was more amused by this than amazed. He knew at first sight where the notion had come from. One of the treaty provisions demanded by Chief Ouray with the main Ute band down in southwestern Colorado had been that the government agree to build a New England–style house for him. It looked like somebody in this bunch didn't want to be outdone by Ouray, not when it came to the niceties. So the Ute got houses while the soldiers lived in tents.

"See, Arm Long?" Pissing Horse chuckled, apparently as amused by the sight as Longarm was. "Soon a town, eh? Need one big sum'bish whorehouse. Then we be a town here. Everybody come. Spend money. All get rich soon." The old man had been back on his own horse ever since they reached the wagon road at the mouth of the canyon and rejoined the other warriors of the welcoming committee.

"What d'you expect t' do for customers in this town of yours, Pissing Horse?"

"Soldier come. Pay for what Indian get free, ha ha. Buy plenty liquor. Get drunk. Spend all money. Good town, Arm Long. All get rich soon."

"You can't put a saloon in here, Pissing Horse. You know that, dammit. I'd have t' come back an' arrest you myself. The law says you can't have liquor."

"No drink, Arm Long. Only sell." The old fart cackled and winked.

Longarm laughed with him. And scratched his chin. What an interesting point Lawyer Able could make out of that one. Federal law was damned well specific in its prohibition of the consumption of alcohol by Indians and the sale of alcohol to them. But did it actually say anything about liquor sales *by* them? Damned if Longarm had an answer to that one right offhand.

Fortunately, it wasn't the sort of thing that would have to be decided here and now.

Even luckier, it wasn't the sort of thing that would have to be decided by Deputy Marshal Custis Long. That, thankfully, he could leave to others. All he might ever have to do about it would be to follow Billy Vail's orders.

In the meantime, well, Pissing Horse already knew that Longarm's views on the subject of Indian alcohol prohibitions were what might be called flexible.

As they rode into the village, the Ute came out to greet their headman and leading warriors. Longarm noticed that some of them apparently weren't quite ready to settle in under shingled roofs. The owners of at least two of the completed houses seemed to be living in brush bowers erected in the yards beside their houses. Maybe they would move inside come winter.

He also noticed that he recognized a fair number of these people. He would have thought he would have forgotten them, but now a good many of them were familiar to him right down to their names.

The girl called Swan most of all. White Swan Floating on Misty Pond at Sunset if he remembered the long way around it.

She hadn't changed much.

Except for the toddler that was nursing at her breast. A toddler, Longarm noticed, that looked almighty pale for a Ute youngster. Surely the kid wasn't . . . no, not likely. Swimming Deer would've mentioned it if that was so. He put that stray notion out of mind.

Swan nodded to him but wasn't any more welcoming than that. Likely she was married now, and while she might remember him, there was nothing in her expression or her eyes to indicate she wanted any resumption of what had been between them before.

Longarm nodded back to her and knew that that was that.

Pissing Horse led the way to a house at the center of the village where a bunch of old men and old women were gathered. The house was neither bigger nor fancier than any of the others, but it was situated like a headman's tepee would have been, centered and with the front door facing the sunrise, so it was probably his.

There was a tall wooden tripod set up on the smallish front porch. The tripod was decorated with feathers and a painted ceremonial drum. And with a good many scalp locks, too. Longarm made a conscious effort to keep from looking to see if any of those scalps were fresher than, say, his last visit to the old headman.

"We eat, Arm Long. Talk to Man in Sky. Then you and Pissing Horse talk, yes?"

"Yes," Longarm agreed.

Talk to Man in Sky, Longarm knew, was a left-handed euphemism for worshiping a very carefully unspecified god. Except the way old Pissing Horse meant it, it really wasn't that, either. What it really was was an excuse. The White Father in Washington said Ute couldn't drink. But the rules also said the Ute were allowed to worship freely. Pissing Horse and some of the other brighter Indians, Ute and otherwise, had figured out that if they mumbled something and said it was a prayer, they could turn the social occasion of getting drunk into a religious ceremony. On the surface of things, anyway. And Longarm was able to go along with that and not have to throw them all in irons for consuming booze where a federal officer could see.

What they did when he wasn't around to see, of course, wasn't all that hard to figure out. Wasn't all that hard to ignore, either, though.

"That man there," Pissing Horse was saying, pointing as he did so, "is father of Bird Talks to the Moon. That man is brother. Now we eat, Arm Long. Talk to Man in Sky. Then talk to that man and that man, eh?"

"I'd like that, Pissing Horse."

The old man called out something in his own language, and the clutch of old women standing by the front door began babbling and running around to get things organized for a blowout.

Longarm put on a fixed smile and his very best company manners and steeled himself to eat any-damn-thing that was put in front of him. Without explanations of what the stuff might be, thank you.

Chapter 21

Longarm was hot. The air inside the hut was stifling. A person would think a brush arbor wouldn't get so stuffy. But this one did. They were seated, practically every male in the band, inside this arbor that had been built next to the front porch of Pissing Horse's frame house. Longarm had no idea why they were here instead of being indoors, where there would have been more room for everybody.

The bowl came his way again, and he drank from it.

Funny. He remembered this stuff as tasting pretty much like chilled dog piss, with maybe some bug guts thrown in for texture. The beverage was something on the order of tiswin or *pulque*. But not so flavorful.

On the other hand it was sneaky. Didn't seem to have any bite to it at all. Until your lips and cheeks and nose turned numb and all of a sudden it was 'most too hot to bear. Right now Longarm was 'most too hot to bear. And the only way he could've been sure he had a nose would've been to reach up and feel of it with both hands. If he could find it, that is.

He felt something cool and damp and most, most welcome on his forehead. He blinked.

There was a girl. Kinda out of focus, but for sure a girl. Swimming Deer? Of course. Had to be Swimming Deer. He grinned. Or tried to.

"Thanksh."

The girl giggled.

What she was doing was wiping his forehead with something cool and wet. Cloth or soft leather. Cold water on it. It felt wonderful.

He hadn't thought women were allowed inside the arbor. He blinked.

91

Funny. The girl wasn't inside the arbor now.

For that matter, neither was Longarm.

He had no notion of how he'd come to get from inside to outside. But he was outside now. Up above he could see starlight. And the girl leaning close to him, the side of her face illuminated by a campfire. There wasn't any fire inside the arbor. No room for one. Besides, a fire in there would've burned the whole shebang down on top of everybody. And wouldn't that be a helluva note. U.S. deputy marshal wiping out a whole band of friendly Indians. Helluva scandal. A guy would have a tough time living that one down. Other deputies would make jokes about him. Longarm wouldn't like that. Prob'ly he shouldn't burn the arbor, then. Not that he was gonna. He was only . . . he was only . . . what in hell *was* he thinking 'bout here? He couldn't remember.

He hiccuped and felt a rush of heat through his belly. Sure felt good, that cool washcloth. Sure did.

Tired. Man, it'd been a long day. He yawned, lost his balance, and nearly toppled over. He felt a supporting hand behind his shoulders, and he smiled.

"You come, Long Long."

He nodded.

He felt himself floating. Only for a second or two. It seemed like his legs were moving, but he wasn't sure about that.

Then he was lying down. There was no transition between the two, no apparent passage of time. Longarm accepted that as perfectly natural. He smiled.

He heard someone snore and thought he might be doing it himself. Not that it mattered.

Warm. It definitely felt warm. But nicely so this time. He could vaguely recall having felt an unpleasant sort of heat sensation earlier, but that had been concentrated in his face and neck. This was quite a different sort of warmth, and it was centered at his groin.

Wherever he was, it was black as tar. No hint of light reached him.

He could smell the faint, aging fragrance of soap and the lighter, drier scent of sun-dried cloth. And something else as well. Something he could almost but not quite remember.

His sense of touch told him that he was lying on a pallet. Not a bed and mattress, he didn't think, but something much more firm than that. A pallet placed on a floor, probably. Whatever stuffing was used in the pallet it was compact now and fairly hard. But not uncomfortable.

There was still that sense of warmth at his groin. Very curious. But also very pleasant.

He felt the first stirrings of an erection in response to the warmth and realized then that he was naked. He was lying under a light cover of some sort but had been completely stripped of his clothing.

That alarmed him for a moment, but when he stirred he felt the solid, comforting lump of steel and leather that he never liked to be farther from than an arm's reach. Whoever undressed him had taken the trouble to wrap his gunbelt around its own holster and lay the holstered Colt next to Longarm's head on the sleeping pallet. He was able to relax after that. Not that he suspected anyone in the Ute band of harboring ill will toward him. But a man never knew. . . .

He relaxed again and once more became conscious of that warmth that was immediately in front of his waist.

Longarm was lying on his right side. The source of the heat was almost close enough to touch.

As his erection became firm, it encountered something there. Something firm but yielding.

And tantalizingly warm and near.

Longarm reached down. His hand found a rounded hip. Rather small but very nicely rounded.

Swimming Deer. He remembered now. Swimming Deer had been there at some point during the wet evening with Pissing Horse and the other men of the band. Swimming Deer had gathered up the pieces and washed him off and somehow brought him here. He smiled.

Longarm gently fondled and stroked the warm womanflesh. Felt small stirrings of response.

He heard a sigh, and the girl's backside pressed itself against his erection.

Longarm grunted and reached around to cup her breast and lightly squeeze it. There was little more than a mouthful of firm flesh there. Her nipple was hard, a warm pebble pressing

93

into the palm of his hand. For some reason it seemed quite wet, too. Sweat, probably. She pushed the covers down to waist level, dragging them away from him at the same time, and then kicked so that they were both free of the cloth or doeskin.

She turned in his arms and faced him. Longarm could feel her breath on his skin, smelled a curious but not unpleasant mixture of onion and mint, tasted then her mouth with that same combination of flavors in it.

He heard her sigh and felt her wriggle happily against him.

"If you—"

"Shhh." She pressed a finger to his lips to shush him. He shrugged and nodded. Then understood. Likely they weren't alone in here, and she was wanting to be careful and not wake whoever else was sleeping nearby.

He felt her pull away from his mouth. Felt the warm, wet, tickling contact of her tongue as she moved down his chest and across his belly.

Damp heat engulfed his cock, and he might have groaned a little.

She draped her arm over his waist and burrowed her face into his crotch.

Longarm's head rolled back as she surrounded him with delectable sensation.

The fingers of one hand teased and tantalized his balls. The nails of her other hand dragged very gently back and forth across the puckered but extraordinarily sensitive rim of his anus. And throughout all that she continued to suck and pull on him while she held his cock inside the eager receptacle of her mouth and throat.

Now this, Longarm concluded, was a damned friendly way for a fella to be treated.

He reached down to her, intending to draw her away so he could turn her over onto her back and mount her. Hell, a guy didn't want to be selfish. But she shook her head vigorously from side to side when he touched her cheek and tried to move her off him. Apparently, she wanted to stay and finish him that way the first time.

Longarm wasn't gonna get mad at her about it. He lay there and let her do as she wished.

94

In fact, if she wanted to do it for the entire remainder of the night, he wouldn't complain too loud.

He smiled and let his eyes sag shut and gave himself over to the sensations she was giving him.

Chapter 22

Longarm's head felt like somebody had spent the previous night packing it with cotton. But other than that he wasn't so bad. Hell, he felt better than most of the Ute men looked this morning.

On the other hand, they might've been at it longer than he managed last night.

He accepted with deep and genuine gratitude the cup of stout, steaming coffee he was handed by a giggly girl of twelve or so.

All the men—all of them that could stand up, anyway—were gathered in a circle outside Pissing Horse's house. Not in the arbor this time, though. Longarm had no idea what determined how the different kinds of dwellings or shelters were used, but for whatever purpose, they were seated in the open air for breakfast.

The women of the band were feeding the menfolk. And doing a whole lot of laughing when they thought no one was looking.

Well, Longarm couldn't blame them. All in all, the men of the crowd, himself included, were a fairly shaky bunch at the moment.

Longarm considered himself lucky that he was feeling really pretty decent. Everything considered.

But then he'd had that nocturnal interlude to get his blood flowing again and help him recuperate.

He looked around for Swimming Deer but didn't see her this morning.

She'd been in a strange damned mood last night. Not that he was complaining. Not hardly. But still and all he would have

96

to say that she'd acted strange. Hadn't wanted him messing in her pussy. She'd wanted him. That was plain enough. Wanted to please him. But she hadn't let him hardly put a finger in her pussy although she hadn't shown any such reluctance back at Camp Brunot. Last night, though, she'd brought him off twice in her mouth and once in her ass but tightened up and pulled away every time he so much as hinted that he wanted to plow the middle field. Weird.

For a bit he'd thought maybe she had started her monthly and didn't want him in there because of that. Then he remembered that that couldn't be so or she wouldn't have been anywhere near him. He had no idea if it was religion or merely custom, but for whatever reason no Indian woman he'd ever known was allowed contact, any sort of contact, with a man when she was on her monthly. They even had to leave their homes and go off into separate, quarantine quarters until the menstrual flow was done with. Something to do with medicine or magic, he thought; a man was supposed to lose all his medicine if so much as the shadow of a menstruating woman touched him.

So Swimming Deer wasn't on her period.

She also wasn't anywhere in sight this morning.

Swan was over on the other side of the circle, bending down to serve choice tidbits to a powerful-looking warrior of thirty or so. Like she'd done before, Swan ignored Longarm today.

He was sorry she seemed to feel that way about him now. There'd been a time when he was awfully fond of Swan. She was pretty. And also one helluva girl for sweating up a bed. Swan was as good at sucking cock as Swimming Deer. And was even wilder than Deer when it came to belly bumping. Once Swan got started, she went purely crazy, yelping and squealing and thrashing around for all she was worth.

That had been a while back, though, and it seemed that things had changed.

Longarm hadn't expected to come wandering in here and pick up where him and Swan left off. Not hardly. She had a kid now and presumably a husband. He wouldn't have wanted to cause any trouble for her. But he still liked her and would've liked a chance to show her that he did.

97

Oh, well. The call was hers to make. He sure wasn't gonna force anything on her that she might not want.

He belched, tasting last night's cactus juice all over again, and hurriedly drank down some coffee to try and get rid of the vile aftertaste. The shit hadn't hardly been drinkable the first time, dammit.

A middle-aged woman leaned over his shoulder and put a bowl into his hands. Longarm wasn't sure what the bowl held. You could make a case for calling it a stew or a soup either one. But that wasn't what worried him. There were bits and pieces of unidentifiable substances lurking in the stuff.

The broth smelled normal enough. It was made from some kind of meat. There were globules of yellowish grease floating on the surface of it, and the steam coming off it smelled good.

But the chunky stuff . . . he probably didn't want to know what any of that was.

He smiled and nodded and thanked the woman.

She laughed and said something to Pissing Horse. The old bastard laughed, too, then winced. That got a round of more laughter from the Indians nearby. Pissing Horse looked as if he thought his head was fixing to split apart, and everybody else was getting a kick out of seeing that.

"Eat, Arm Long. Feel better." Pissing Horse took his own advice, gulping down huge mouthfuls of the stew, barely pausing for breath and then gulping another. Grease ran down his chin and onto his chest, and still he drank and chewed and snorted until his bowl was empty. Then he held the bowl over his shoulder for the nearest woman to take and refill.

Longarm followed Pissing Horse's advice, although not with quite so much gusto. Fortunately, the stuff didn't taste half as nasty as it looked. In fact, it tasted pretty good. There was mutton somewhere in there, he thought. But not so strong as to gag anybody. Maybe some sort of liver. A couple different kinds of roots and grains, something else that looked like boiled weeds. He suspected part of it was ration-issue goods and part the locally available native foods.

"Good, yes?"

"Good," Longarm agreed. He had a little more to help prove the point.

"Big talk las' night, Arm Long."

"Big talk," he agreed again. Lordy, he hoped they hadn't talked about anything serious last night. Because if they had, well, he had no damned recollection of it now.

"You send Bird Talks home, Arm Long."

"I never promised you no such thing, Pissing Horse." He hoped. No, dammit, he was sure he hadn't. He couldn't have. Not even passing out drunk would he make a promise that stupid.

"Send home," Pissing Horse insisted.

"Only if I can. T' tell you the truth, Pissing Horse, it looks t' me like he's guilty. Might be the best thing for him if they leave things like they are, y' know. If this thing was t' come to trial, Bird Talks to the Moon could end up hanging. That wouldn't be good."

"No hang. Spirit cannot rest if hang, Arm Long. We tell you all this las' night, eh? No hang. Send home, yes?"

"You're a fair man, Pissing Horse. If Bird Talks to the Moon is guilty of what they say—"

"No!" Pissing Horse bellowed, causing the whole damn circle to go quiet and start looking at him and Longarm.

"I only meant—"

"That man's son could *not* do. We tell you this, Arm Long."

Longarm looked across the circle at the father of the army scout who now was accused of murder.

It's one damn thing to face a killer. It's quite another to have to see the mother and the father after the killer has been brought to justice. That was something Longarm never had liked. He would much rather face two men with guns than one gray-haired mother with tears in her eyes.

"Nobody wants to hang him," he said. It was the only comfort he could think of to offer.

"Remember what we say," Pissing Horse told him.

Longarm damn sure hoped the old man was referring to the things that had been said just now. Because he still couldn't recall shit from last night.

Thinking to change the subject, he took another swallow of the good coffee—which just might've saved his life, he thought—and asked, "Where's Swimming Deer this morning?"

Pissing Horse frowned. "Swimming Deer? She work for sojer at fort, Arm Long."

"Yeah, I know that."

"Not here, Arm Long. Stay at fort. Too far to walk every day, an' Swimming Deer got no horse. Too far even on horse. She live there now. Come home someday soon. Not now."

It was Longarm's turn to frown. If Swimming Deer wasn't in the village last night, then who . . . ?

He looked around the circle.

There were plenty of women here. Women and girls who ranged in age from eight to eighty were serving breakfast to the men. Pretty ones. Ugly ones. Tall and short ones, skinny and fat ones. Every female in the band, he guessed.

And not a single damned one of them was paying any particular attention to Deputy Marshal Custis Long this morning.

So who the hell . . . ?

He felt his cheeks go hot and was fairly sure his ears and neck were flushed. He hoped nobody noticed.

Now that he thought about it, dammit, Swimming Deer's tits were soft and fluid. Last night he'd touched firm flesh.

And the girl last night had a smaller waist than Swimming Deer, too.

But who . . . ?

If it made him feel any better—and once he thought about it, he acknowledged that it did—the girl, or woman, last night hadn't been at any really strange extreme of age. She'd been old enough to have tits but not so old that her tits turned into porridge.

That was something.

He supposed.

For the remainder of the breakfast meal Longarm found himself staring at the women and the girls who were serving the meal. Trying to work out by way of a look, a gesture, a smile—just any way at all—which one of them had been in his bed through the wee hours.

He never caught so much as a clue.

Chapter 23

Longarm bent forward to hold a match for Pissing Horse, lighting the cheroot Longarm had just given him. Then he lighted his own and leaned back with a sigh of contentment. He felt better now. The breakfast had helped some, the coffee even more. Hell, he was beginning to think now that he might survive all the way past noon.

"Tell me, Grandfather . . ." he began. The question he intended to ask was cut off by the loud clatter of hoofbeats coming in at a dead run.

A Ute boy of fourteen or so—no doubt he would have described himself as a full-fledged warrior—rode a sweat-lathered pony into the midst of the houses and barely took time to slow the animal before he dropped off its back into a run that carried him into the circle of people. The boy was as breathless as if he'd been the one doing the running instead of the horse.

Forgetting himself for the moment, he tried to rush straight across the circle. One of the older warriors grabbed him by the arm and held him back. The boy mumbled an apology and backed out of the circle, running around the outside of it to reach Pissing Horse's side. Longarm vaguely recalled that it would have been a breach of etiquette for anyone to cut straight through the middle.

The boy burst into a torrent of babble, his tongue tripping all over itself in his rush to get the words out. He was speaking his own language naturally enough, but whatever he said was something that captured the attention of every Indian around.

Pissing Horse turned rigid, and the circle dissolved as the Ute, men and women alike, crowded around to hear what the boy was saying.

101

"What is it?" Longarm asked. Several times. No one was interested in answering just then.

A few of the men, substantial warriors for the most part, turned away before all the story was told. Grimly they marched off. Longarm had no idea what tale they were hearing. But he recognized their manner. They had the look of men who were about to arm themselves and go looking for blood trouble.

Pissing Horse questioned the boy briefly. So did the man who was Bird Talks to the Moon's father. Then Bird's father left the group, also, and Pissing Horse gave Longarm a worried look.

"What is it, dammit?" Longarm demanded.

"Bad, Arm Long. Bad."

"Bird Talks?"

Pissing Horse nodded. "Dead yes or no. Old lootnant kill him yes or no. Bird Talks dead now maybe yes, maybe no."

"Shit," Longarm muttered.

Pissing Horse solemnly nodded again, as if Longarm had just said something wise.

"At Camp Brunot this was?" Longarm asked. "Just now?"

Pissing Horse nodded. "Keep a watch there. The boy see this happen. Old lootnant have Bird Talk tied. Beat him. Kill him maybe yes, maybe no. If Bird Talk is dead now, we will fight, Arm Long. You always tell us, sojer always tell us, you damn Ute, you learn white way. Fair trial. Nobody done wrong till trial he say so. Huh. No damn trial for Bird Talk, Arm Long. No damn trail when sojer don' want to be bothered by damn Ute, eh? Is true, Arm Long. If Bird Talk is dead now, we will dance. Paint. Make war. More of you than Ute. You whites will win. But we give you one hell'a fight for a time, eh? Wipe out damn sojer at fort this time. Do like stinking damn Lakota an' run for land of the grandmother, eh? This time we fight fast an' run away quick. Maybe even win, eh?" He cackled.

Damned if the old bastard didn't sound like he meant it, too. If the "old lootnant"—that would pretty much have to be deNunzio since Longarm wasn't entirely sure that Willis was old enough to've started shaving yet—had killed Bird Talks to the Moon, then Pissing Horse's band was gonna do their best to massacre all the bluecoat soldiers at Camp Brunot and then make a run for the border with the Grandmother's Land, known to whites as Canada.

It occurred to Longarm, not for the first time, that the grandmother, old Queen Victoria, and her redcoat Mounties did some things better than Uncle Sam and his bluecoats ever managed. Dealing with Indians came first and foremost to mind in that regard.

The biggest difference in treatment that Longarm had noticed—oh, other than that the redcoats didn't so often shoot at first sight of an Indian—was that the Grandmother's people seemed t'have this crazy notion that Indians ought to be treated fair. That was an idea that had never much caught on on the south side of the border.

Longarm scowled and drew on his cheroot. "Don't put the paint on just on the say-so of a boy, Pissing Horse."

"Red Beaver not a liar, Arm Long. Not—"

"Hell, that isn't what I'm saying, dammit. All I'm telling you is that you don't have all the facts yet. Maybe something— oh, I don't know . . . maybe things aren't the way they seem, that's all. What I'm asking you to do is wait and see what the truth is before you start a war over it. Let me find out for you. Would you do that, Pissing Horse? Would you trust me to find out if Bird Talks is still alive and what happened that he was beaten by the old lieutenant? Would you do that, please?"

Pissing Horse frowned. Kneaded his face with the bony fingers of one hand. Turned his head and spat. Mumbled something to one of the men who was standing beside him. "You would warn damn sojer, Arm Long. Tell them we come to fight."

Longarm looked the old headman in the eyes. "If it comes to that, Pissing Horse, yes. I will tell them."

Pissing Horse nodded, satisfied. He would have expected no less. It was only the lie of a denial that would have destroyed his confidence in Arm Long.

"You come here to help us."

"Yes, I did."

"Now you help sojer."

"I don't know, Pissing Horse. I can't know what I'll do until I find out what happened between the old lieutenant and Bird Talks to the Moon."

"You will come back here? Even if you know we will fight after you talk to us?"

"I can promise you that much, yes."

Pissing Horse nodded abruptly. "Go. We will wait. But not long. We wait"—the old man turned and engaged in a brief conversation with several of the other warriors—"three day. You come back in three day, Arm Long. Then we will talk. Won' fight for three day, though. My word on this."

"And my word that I'll be back here within three days, Pissing Horse."

Three days, Longarm reflected as he turned away. There would be some significance to that. Pissing Horse didn't just pull the figure out of a hat.

Then Longarm thought he knew. It was only a guess, of course. But he suspected it hit the mark. Three days would be how long it would take the Utes to arm themselves fully. Probably they were short on ammunition and needed three days to reach some town or outpost where they could stock up on cartridges and whatever other supplies they might need.

That damned old Pissing Horse was no fool. He was willing to grant Longarm a favor. And then use it to his own advantage. Well, no hard feelings. He was entitled.

Longarm just hoped he could use the three days to find out what the hell was going on here.

Swan, who spoke English about as well as Longarm did and who had been among those listening in on the conversations, both the one with the boy named Red Beaver and then the one between Pissing Horse and Longarm, hurried away and was back moments later leading Longarm's government-issue horse. The pretty girl managed to hand him the reins without ever once looking directly at him.

Longarm had no time at the moment, though, to think about White Swan Floating on Misty Pond at Sunset.

Right now he was somewhat more interested in stopping a war between the Ute nation and the United States of America.

He swung onto his saddle and took a moment to adjust the set of his Stetson, then looked down at the Ute who were clustered close around his stirrups. "Three days," he affirmed to Pissing Horse. "I'll be back in that time either way."

Pissing Horse said something in his own language and raised a hand in farewell as Longarm reined the horse toward the road back to Camp Brunot and Second Lieutenant Raphael deNunzio.

Chapter 24

Good Lord, it was an awful good thing that it was only a lone deputy marshal who was riding in from the Ute town at the moment and not a howling, hot-blooded war party.

Longarm stopped his horse on the road so he could cup his hands around a match and get a cheroot alight. While he did so, he stared at Camp Brunot and marveled at how open and unprepared an entire garrison of United States Army troops could allow themselves to become.

The soldiers had no faint notion that the Ute were at the boiling point and fixing to go to war.

In front of Longarm right now there were dozens of tents, scores of work parties, construction crews, teamsters, cooks, bakers, laundresses . . . shit, the list was endless. Or nearly so. There were a few significant possibilities that seemed to be missing here.

Guards, for instance. The only guards Longarm could see were the one who stood outside the guard tent at the edge of the camp and, over in the middle of things, the one other guard that was posted outside Clytemnestra Benhurst's tent.

Except for those two fellows, though, there seemed to be no attention being paid to any need for security. Hell, except for those two guards there weren't even any rifles in sight at the moment. Hammers, hods, and trowels, sure, but not rifles.

Under the circumstances that seemed foolishness on Lieutenant Willis's part. To the point of criminal stupidity considering what deNunzio'd been up to this morning.

Longarm frowned and rode forward. No one paid the least bit of attention to his return.

First Lieutenant Henry Willis gestured in the air with his right hand as if shooing a fly. What he was actually brushing aside, however, was Custis Long's concerns about the depth of feelings being experienced by the Ute.

"Nothing to it," Willis said. "Absolutely nothing to it, man. There couldn't be, you see, or I would have been told. And no such incident has been reported. Therefore, quid pro quorum, there has been no such incident, Marshal. You needn't concern yourself."

Quid pro quo . . . oh. Willis was trying to talk fancy. And fucking it up. What he wanted was whatever longhair Latin words it stood for when somebody wrote down *i.e.* Longarm had no idea what *i.e.* stood for. But it wasn't no quid pro quorum, he was sure 'bout that. And Henry Willis didn't know, neither. Longarm chewed on the end of his cheroot and wondered just how dumb Willis really was.

"You see," Willis was going on now, "civilians really shouldn't involve themselves in matters like this. The army understands Indians and Indian problems, Marshal. It would serve us all to best advantage if you simply go on about your job of catching this train robber fellow you were telling me about and leave my Ute alone. Come to think of it, what were you doing over there bothering them?"

"Firstly, Lieutenant, I don't know as I was bothering them. I went over there to see an old friend. A visit, like. So I happen to've been there and seen how upset they got this morning when they heard that Bird Talks to the Moon was beaten and maybe killed."

"Rumor. Nothing but rumor, Marshal."

"Something you oughta think about, Lieutenant. Leaving aside for the moment the question o' what's true and what ain't in this here particular situation, a rumor that's believed can start a war just as quick as a truth will."

Willis frowned.

"An' as for civilians messing about with 'your' Indians, it seems I recall something about a civilian commission having charge o' Indian affairs nowadays. So while we're on the subject, where is the agent for this here reservation? Come t' that, dammit, where's the reservation? All I seen so far is fort and village. No sign yet o' any agent or agency headquarters."

"The appropriate agency has not yet seen fit to establish a headquarters," Willis said. "I understand that an agent has been assigned, but he hasn't shown up yet. Until or unless he does, sir, it is the United States Army in charge here. Not the Justice Department. I do want you to remember that."

"Oh, I remember it all right. I also remember what it was that brung me back here in a big hurry. Those Ute are mad, Willis. They're fighting mad. Their man has been beat by Lieutenant deNunzio, and the Ute don't like it."

"He has not—"

"Ask him."

"What?"

"I said call the man in here an' ask him. That isn't s' much, is it? You say he didn't do it, so fine, bring him in an' let me hear him say that he didn't."

"I shan't consider any such thing."

"You afraid o' what you'll hear if you start asking questions, Willis?"

"Nonsense. I shan't dignify these accusations by responding to them, that's all. Believe me, I shall not fall into the trap of getting a-dither every time some filthy Ute passes wind. I recommend you learn to do the same. And I also recommend that you go about your business, Marshal. I suggest you concentrate on . . . What was his name again?"

"Cletus Bacon," Longarm said. "Wanted for mail theft. I believe I told you that a'ready."

"Yes. So you did." Willis's smile said he'd remembered the name right along. He'd been trying to trap Longarm into showing a lie by himself forgetting the fictitious name of the criminal he was supposed to be looking for here.

"About these Ute, though, Willis, I think you oughta know—"

"I don't want to hear any more on this subject, Marshal. I really don't. The record of this regiment is second to none when it comes to Indian affairs, Marshal. Our experience dates back longer than you or I either one has been alive. I assure you, sir, we know how to deal with it."

"*Your* experience don't go back any further than, what? A couple weeks? Couple months at the most, Willis? So what kinda—"

The officer cut him short, then stood and gave Longarm a curt nod of dismissal, not bothering this time to offer his hand to shake. "I have official duties to attend to, Marshal, and no more time for this nonsense. Please do not bother me again with any more of those Indians' hysteria."

Longarm shuddered. To think that a guy like this could actually be in charge here, responsible for the lives of hundreds of soldiers and Indians, too. . . . Now, wasn't that a scary notion, indeed.

"Good day, Lieutenant." He turned and marched out of the headquarters tent.

Chapter 25

Henry Willis didn't want to ask Raphael deNunzio about what happened this morning? Fine. Longarm would go and ask the man about it himself.

If nothing else, maybe he could at least convince *one* of the two commissioned officers at Camp Brunot that they had a genuinely serious Indian problem brewing.

"You can generally find the adjutant somewhere around the construction area, sir," a baby-faced soldier wearing canvas fatigues and carrying an empty bucket told him. "Either over there somewhere, sir, or else in the officers' mess supervising the cooks."

"Thanks." Longarm headed toward the busy flat where foundations and stonework floors were being laid preparatory to the construction of permanent buildings for Brunot. It was impossible to tell at this point what the buildings would be. But there were going to be an awful lot of them, all laid out in precise rows. The area was crisscrossed with stakes and taut twine to show where walls and corners should be.

"No, sir, not this morning," a lean corporal told him. "I ain't seen Lieutenant DeNunzio yet t'day." He turned his head and spat a stream of brown juice into the batch of mortar that two sweating privates were mixing. "An' now that I think of it, it's mighty odd that I haven't. Most gener'ly he's underfoot somewhere around here near all the time. But I hain't seen hide nor hair of him yet t'day, sir. Sorry."

A sergeant whose energies seemed mostly concentrated on growing a truly magnificent mustache was somewhat more candid on the subject. "Nope. Ain't seen him. Don't wanta see him. Finally able to get some work done around here without Mr. deNunzio telling the boys the way he wants things done.

110

So if you see 'im, mister, don't you be telling him to hurry back an' supervise my people, you hear? Whatever he's found to keep hisself busy today, don't you go and pull him away from it."

"Could you tell me where the officers' mess is, please? I can't seem to keep all these tents straight in my mind."

The sergeant grunted and pointed.

"Thanks." Longarm walked off in that direction.

"Nope. Not today, thank goodness."

"He usually comes in here, though?" Longarm asked.

"That's for damn sure. Every morning. Except this one, that is. Comes in and wants to go over the menu with me. And believe me, whatever it is that I've got planned, he has something else in mind. Hell, I keep asking him to go ahead an' set the menu himself, but he won't do it. Says that isn't an officer's responsibility. Now I ask you."

Longarm smiled and shrugged.

"Yeah. Easy for you to say."

The smile turned into a grin.

The mess sergeant grinned, too, then and hooked a thumb over his shoulder. "I got coffee nice and fresh if you'd want some, sir. Or I could fix you up a little something to tide you over to suppertime. Got some antelope I could slice for sandwiches or some partridge left over from dinner. It's cold but oughta go down nice enough with a little wine to help it slide down the gullet better."

"I'm fine, thanks."

The mess sergeant, who looked like he already had thirty years' service behind him and expected to put in at least that number again, looked disappointed.

"I'm too busy to take the time right now," Longarm said, relenting for the sake of the man's pride, "but maybe I could come back later when I have a minute?"

"Any time, sir. Believe me, with only two officers on the post at the moment, well, my people aren't exactly overworked, sir. Even if one of them officers is Lieutenant deNunzio, if you'll forgive me for saying it. Anyway, any time you want a bite to eat, sir, you just let me know what you have in mind, and I'll see can't I come up with it."

111

"Mighty kind of you, Sergeant."

"Be my pleasure, sir."

"Do you, uh, have any idea where Lieutenant deNunzio might be this morning, Sergeant?"

"No, sir. Sorry."

Longarm shrugged and thanked the man, then turned and started out of the kitchen tent.

"Psst. Long Long."

He stopped. Swimming Deer and another Ute girl whom Longarm recognized as one of the girls who served in the officers' mess were standing at the side of the kitchen tent. If they had bothered to listen in, they would have heard Longarm's conversation with the mess sergeant easily through the cloth wall.

It occurred to him that Swimming Deer really was still here at Camp Brunot. So she couldn't have been the one who came in to join him in his bed last night. That incident had been more than just pleasant. But it sure was still a puzzlement, too.

He smiled and walked over to her, not sure if she would welcome a show of affection with someone else looking on but certainly not wanting to ignore her here. "Hello, Swimming Deer."

"Hello, Long Long. Did you miss me las' night?"

"Very much," he lied.

"You want me tonight, Long Long?" Either she didn't mind the other girl knowing, or the second girl didn't speak any English.

"I'd be pleased, Swimming Deer."

She grinned and nodded, then said something to the other girl and pointed at Longarm's crotch. The second girl's eyes went wide, and she clapped a hand over her mouth to try and hide her amazement. This second girl gave Longarm an impish look and said something in her own tongue. Obviously, she was making a joke of some sort, but Swimming Deer didn't appreciate it. Swimming Deer got pissed and snapped something back at the girl, then stuck her nose into the air and took Longarm's elbow with a haughty sniff. She practically dragged him away from that other girl, leading him off in the direction of the parade ground.

"You sure you don't speak Ute, Long Long?"

"Not a word of it."

"Good."

He laughed. "Whatever she said, Swimming Deer, it wouldn't have made any difference. You're a lot prettier than she is."

Swimming Deer giggled and preened. "You think?"

"I know."

"Prettier 'an Swan, too?"

"You're much prettier." That might not be the true thing to say. But it was by far the wiser of the two possible answers to that question.

Swimming Deer seemed satisfied. She gave his elbow a squeeze and pressed her cheek against his shoulder for a moment while she swayed at his side, her steps timed to his so that they moved comfortably together. "You look for Lootnant Nunzie, Long Long?"

"Yes, but he doesn't seem to be in any of his usual places today, Swimming Deer."

"Lootnant Nunzie with that woman, Long Long." Swimming Deer made a face like she'd just gotten a whiff of something distasteful.

"What woman, Swimming Deer?"

"You know, Long Long. We call her Two Face Woman. She is old major's woman. One they say Bird Talks to Moon take." Swimming Deer turned her head and spat. "Bird, he more smarter than that, Long Long. Pah."

"Mrs. Benhurst?" Longarm asked.

Swimming Deer glowered. And nodded. "Lootnant Nunzie, he is with Two Face Woman."

Longarm wondered what Sly had done to make Swimming Deer hate her so.

Then he realized. Of course. And it was simple human nature at work here. Human nature that in this case would have nothing at all to do with Sly Benhurst herself.

The explanation was that Bird Talks to the Moon went overboard with rage and lust when he saw Mrs. Benhurst. He murdered three men and kidnapped and raped the major's wife. Never mind that nobody actually is going to be crazed by passion at the sight of a woman. *Any* woman, no matter how attractive she might be. What Longarm understood but the Ute likely did not was that whatever it was that had been brewing inside Bird Talks to the Moon had been brewing there for a good long time before the day Mrs. Benhurst became the last straw and Bird Talks snapped. The point as Swimming Deer and the rest of the Ute would see it was that Mrs. Benhurst was the trigger and therefore should be held somehow at fault. They probably would believe that Bird Talks to the Moon never would have gone round the bend like he did if it hadn't been for Sly Benhurst showing up where and when she did, and therefore, she was at least partially guilty for Bird Talks's crimes.

As a line of reasoning, that view was seriously flawed. But on a gut response level it was damn well inescapable. Of course Swimming Deer would despise Sly now. All the Ute would. They were virtually forced to if they cared anything at all for Bird Talks to the Moon.

Longarm realized there was no point in trying to talk Swimming Deer out of her conviction that Sly was to blame. The Ute girl's feelings were natural. And harmless. Instead, he let that slide and gave Swimming Deer's hand a squeeze. "I hope you'll have time to come, uh, visit with me tonight. I've missed you."

That pleased her.

"For now, though, I have to go talk to Lieutenant deNunzio, Swimming Deer. Thanks for telling me where I can find him."

"You stay away from Two Face Woman, Long Long."

"I'm just going over there to talk to Lieutenant deNunzio, Swimming Deer."

"Hokay." She smiled and let go of his hand, then ran back toward the officers' mess with a childish hop and skip in her step.

Longarm paused for a moment to get his bearings, then angled off in the direction of the guarded tent where Sly was staying. It occurred to him that Swimming Deer expressed no anger at Raphael deNunzio just now. So she hadn't heard anything about the lieutenant beating Bird Talks to the Moon half to death earlier. Or possibly more than half.

Did that mean that Willis was right, that there really hadn't been any such incident despite what Red Beaver told the tribe?

Lordy, Longarm hoped this whole thing was nothing but a young boy's misunderstanding.

He quickened his pace, all the more anxious now to talk to Raphael deNunzio and see if he couldn't get this thing cleared up.

He had enough on his plate right now without adding an Indian war to the difficulties of the moment.

Chapter 26

"Halt, sir. Or I'll shoot."

"Dammit, Abner, it's me. I was here just yesterday, remember?"

"I know that, sir, but I have my orders. If you come any closer, I'll shoot."

Damned if Sly Benhurst's pet sentry didn't sound serious about that, Longarm conceded. Not happy about it, mind, but serious nonetheless.

"All right, Abner, I won't come no closer. Whyn't you please tell Miz Benhurst that I've come to call on her, um? I won't move till you get back."

"Yes, sir." Abner executed a snappy about-face, shouldered his rifle, and marched, actually marched, the four paces it took for him to reach the front of the widow's tent. Once there he still didn't relax. He brought the heavy Springfield down to port arms, coughed loudly, and reached out to go through the formality of "knocking" on the tent pole. The canvas flaps, Longarm noticed, were tied shut even though the midday sun likely was turning the interior of the windowless tent into a pretty fair substitute for an oven. "Caller to see the lady," Abner announced in a voice that just might have been strong enough to carry out to the Ute town.

Oddly enough, Longarm could see the front of the tent wrinkle and sag a bit as an edge of a flap was tugged back just far enough for somebody to peep out. Then it fell back the way it had been.

Abner in the meantime had returned to a position of attention and made another about-face so that he was posed with his back to the tent, and his rifle, bayonet mounted, was ready at his side. The youngster surely was doing things by the book today.

Longarm wasn't sure but thought he heard voices from inside the tent. More than one in a whispered but rasping and probably angry conversation. He decided he must've come at a bad time. Interrupted a lunch? Maybe. But why with the tent closed up? Not that it was any of his business, of course.

He lighted a cheroot and gave Abner a wink that the sentry pretended not to see. It occurred to Longarm that Sly Benhurst might be a little peeved with him today. What with one thing and another yesterday it had completely slipped his mind that he'd promised to have supper with her last night. And there'd been, um, certain other intimations as well. Or so he'd kind of thought at the time. Well, none of that had worked out. He'd have to explain, though, once she decided to come out an' talk. Wouldn't be at all polite to ignore his oversight. Better to admit to it and apologize and let that be the end of it.

Damn, now that he was thinking about promises made but not yet kept, there were a whole bunch of drinks he was owing. To those teamsters who'd brought him here, to Sergeant Hendricks, who determined how a man was mounted around here . . . hell, there were likely others he owed but couldn't call to mind right now, too. First chance he got he was gonna have to make amends for all of that. But for right now business had to come first. And that meant stopping a small war. He cleared his throat and wondered if Abner would enjoy a cheroot. Prob'ly not, judging from the way the boy was acting today. He hadn't been so tight yesterday, but now he sure was. Later, maybe. Longarm flicked the ash off his smoke and watched it shatter and disappear as it fluttered earthward and struck a pebble.

He was downright positive he could hear voices inside that tent now. Louder than before. And definitely pissed off. Sly Benhurst's voice sounding kinda weepy and whining. And a man's much deeper tones sounding madder and madder. The louder she got, the madder the man got.

Longarm could see that Abner was commencing to turn red around the neck and ears. But then Abner was closer to the tent. He'd be able to hear what they were saying inside while Longarm could only catch a word every now and then. Whatever was being said in there, the boy wasn't wanting to hear it. He fidgeted and began to sweat.

117

"I've come at a bad time," Longarm suggested. "Perhaps you oughta tell Mrs. Benhurst that I'll call on her later. Meantime, Abner, I need to see Lieutenant deNunzio. Got any idea where I might be able to find him?"

The young sentry gave Longarm a stricken look. His jaw dropped open, but he gaped and swallowed like a banked fish sucking air.

Longarm understood then. Lieutenant deNunzio was inside that tent with Sly Benhurst. It was the two of them that Longarm'd interrupted.

Well, there wasn't any harm done. They were two grown folks and entitled to do what they pleased.

"Never mind, Abner," Longarm said smoothly. "If you, um, happen t' see the lieutenant later on t'day, please tell 'im I need to speak with him."

"Y-yes, sir."

Longarm smiled and started to turn away.

Just as he did so, the front flap of the tent was yanked aside, and Raphael deNunzio barged out into the glare of the sunshine.

The officer's tunic was buttoned to the throat, but Longarm could see that he was shirtless under it. He was hatless as well, and his slightly greasy-looking dark curls were tangled in wild disarray. He looked like a man who had just gotten out of bed. As no doubt he had.

He was wearing no sash or pistol belt, but in his left hand he was brandishing a sword. Not some crude cavalry saber or fancily engraved ceremonial dress blade, either, but a genuine sword of the sort that gentlemen and officers used to fight with back when sharp steel was both more common and more reliable than gunpowder.

"You!" deNunzio bellowed.

"Me?" Longarm asked.

"Cad."

"Who?"

"Coward."

"Whoa, now."

"You, sir, are no gentleman."

Longarm shrugged. Whatever bee was in Raphael de-Nunzio's bonnet right now, Longarm wanted no part of it.

"Whyn't we talk after you sober up, Raphael?"

"I challenge you."

"Huh?"

"Unless you are a coward, sir, I expect to see you on the field of honor. The engagement shall occur immediately following retreat, sir. Have your second discuss the arrangements with Sergeant Major Gompert. The sergeant major will act as my second." DeNunzio gave Longarm a chilling look, then came to attention and snapped a sword salute that was as rigid and proper as anything Longarm'd ever seen.

Longarm refused to be intimidated by this posturing sonofabitch. Instead of rising to all the bait deNunzio was throwing around, Longarm grinned and said, "Mighty good, Lieutenant, mighty good salute there. Why, I seen fellas cut their noses clean off their faces tryin' t' do that. An' all you done was t' slice off a few nose hairs. Mind, though, they don't look all that nice layin' on the blue o' your coat. Out o' place there, if you see what I mean. You might oughta brush them off lest they ruin the effect o' what you're tryin' to get acrost." He touched his hat brim, first in Abner's direction, then toward deNunzio. "Bye, fellas." He started away, then turned back as if he'd just remembered something. "Don't forget, Raphael, I need t' talk t' you quick as you're sober enough to make some sense." He smiled again and left.

Chapter 27

"Come in." Longarm was inside his tent—the make-believe visiting officers' quarters tent that had been erected out of the way for him, that is—with his shirt off and a basin of tepid water on the stand in front of him. There was no provision for bathing, so he was doing the best he could. For the rest of it he would simply have to settle for a shave and a change into clean linen and the knowledge that no one else around here seemed any better off. The facilities at Camp Brunot were spartan.

"Sir!"

He turned to see Sergeant Major Gompert standing stiffly to attention just inside Longarm's tent. "Sit down, Sergeant. No need t' be formal here."

Gompert acted like he hadn't heard. The man did not even unbend enough to go to a parade-rest stance.

"Suit yourself," Longarm mumbled. He draped his washcloth over the edge of the water basin, then picked up his soap mug and shaving brush, churning vigorously at the soap to build a lather. He stood with his back to Gompert and looked into the polished-steel field mirror that was hanging from a tack driven into a tent pole.

Gompert cleared his throat. Longarm continued to ignore the man. He was beginning to decide that the sergeant major was as big an ass as the adjutant on this post. They were both picky-prissy pricks as far as Longarm could tell. He wet his face and lathered it, then fetched a razor out of his flat traveling case and gave it a few strokes on the strop while the wet lather softened his whiskers. If Gompert wanted to stand back there like an organ-grinder's monkey, he was welcome to do so; Longarm was going on with life in the meantime.

"Sir," Gompert said finally.

"Mmm?" Longarm eyed himself in the mirror, used the ball of his thumb to stretch the skin taut, and drew the straight-edged razor swiftly down his cheek. He wiped the blade on a hand towel, then made another sure stroke.

"Lieutenant deNunzio is still expecting your answer, sir," Gompert said in a voice so crisp it was unnatural.

"Izzat so?" Longarm asked mildly. He began to shave under his jaw, leaving the delicate maneuvering around the nose for last.

"It is, sir."

"Funny thing, Sergeant. I'm still expecting the lieutenant t' show up here so's me and him can talk. The way I see it, mister, what he has in mind is a private affair. T' say nothing 'bout it being illegal, too. What I'm tryin' t' handle is official business of the government him and me both work for." He wiped his razor blade clean of lather and bits of whisker and began shaving around his nose, tugging this way and that and screwing his face into odd contortions as he went. This part of the daily chore was best handled by a barber. But even if there had been a barber at Camp Brunot, Longarm wasn't sure he would've trusted him.

"I wouldn't know anything about that, sir," Gompert said sternly.

"Nope. Neither will the lieutenant 'less he bothers t' ask," Longarm pointed out. He used a few feather-light strokes with the tip of the razor to finish his shave and then began cleaning things up. Not bad, he told himself. He felt a mite tender here and there, but there wasn't any blood seeping anyplace. Not bad at all.

"I've been asked to secure your response, sir," Gompert persisted.

"Damn if he ain't serious about this," Longarm said.

"Entirely serious, sir."

"I don't have time for bullshit, Sergeant."

"None is intended, sir."

"Tell Lieutenant deNunzio, please, that I will be glad to discuss his, uh, challenge. But only after both of us 've met our official duties."

"That would have to wait, sir. This is a matter of honor."

Longarm finished wiping the excess lather from his face.

He tossed the towel down and turned to face the rigidly posed sergeant major. "Honor supposed to take precedent over duty, is it?"

Gompert held himself even more stiffly upright than before, a feat that Longarm would've sworn couldn't have been possible if he hadn't seen it for himself. "Sir," the sergeant major snapped, "honor is precedent over *any*thing else. Even duty. Sir."

"Tell me, Sergeant Major," Longarm guessed. "Have you been an officer yourself? Like sometime in the past maybe?"

"That is irrelevant. Sir."

Longarm grunted.

"What response may I give to the lieutenant, sir?"

"I got work t' do here, Sergeant Major. I got no time for some blue-belly poppinjay's games."

"The lieutenant is playing no game, sir. He is deadly serious."

"Dammit, man, he's serious about *what*? I don't even know what dishonorable thing I'm s'posed to've done to get him so riled."

"You would have to discuss that with the lieutenant, sir."

"Fine. Tell the silly sonofabitch to come around. We'll talk about that. Right after we talk about things like the Ute Indian tribe going to war with the United States Army. Because of Lieutenant Raphael deNunzio, I might add. Personally, Sergeant Major, I'm a whole lot more interested in worrying 'bout that than I am in answering some stupid challenge on an alleged field of honor."

"I can assure you, sir, that Lieutenant deNunzio will not consider anything you have to say until or unless he obtains satisfaction from you."

"And if one o' us is dead afterward?"

Gompert damn near smiled. "Then that party will not have to concern himself with the Ute situation. Sir."

Longarm rolled his eyes. "And if neither of us dies?"

"That would not matter, sir. Not if honor is satisfied."

"We could quit this horseshit and get down to business if the challenge thing is disposed of?"

"I can assure you of that, sir."

Longarm fingered his chin. "All right, dammit. Immediately

after retreat. In the swale just t'other side of the tent where Bird Talks to the Moon is being held."

"Very good, sir. Will you need assistance in securing a second?"

"Nope. Got somebody in mind a'ready."

"Very well, sir. Will it be satisfactory for Lieutenant deNunzio to arrange for the services of an attending physician? Or would you prefer to secure your own?"

"Anybody he wants will be fine with me."

"Yes, sir. Have you your own swords, sir?"

"I do not."

"The lieutenant is able to provide those, also, sir."

"Bottom of the swale, Sergeant Major. Right after retreat. Okay?"

"Very good, sir."

"And tell Raphael that I'll want t' have a long talk with him afterward. It's important."

"I will convey your message, sir. Although the availability of both parties will depend upon, um—"

"Yes, I understand that, Sergeant Major. I wouldn't expect the lieutenant to make any firm promises that he might not be able t' keep. Tell him I do understand that the commitment is, uh, tentative."

"Tentative. I am sure the lieutenant will appreciate your use of that word, sir. And I know he looks forward to your meeting later."

"Yeah. Just make sure he knows he's obligated t' have that talk with me after, Sergeant Major. If it works out that the both of us can, that is."

"Yes, sir. Very good, sir. Good day, sir." Gompert had been standing like a bronze statue throughout the conversation. Now he snapped a salute, made an about-face, and marched out into the late-afternoon sunshine.

Longarm shook his head. What assholes. Still . . . He yawned and leaned down to retrieve his vest from where he'd laid it at the foot of his cot. He pulled his Ingersoll out of the watch pocket and checked the time. There were several things he needed to do before it was time to hike out to Raphael deNunzio's field of honor. He hoped he had time enough to get everything done.

Chapter 28

Retreat really wasn't a very sensible time to be thinking of starting a duel, Longarm reflected as he sat on a slab of gritty rock and chewed the end of an unlighted cheroot. Retreat was sounded at sundown. Or, more accurately, was sounded at whatever time the local commander *thought* was sundown. On an out-of-the-way post like Camp Brunot, that could be anything within three-quarters of an hour of the actual disappearance of the sun.

A really hardnosed commander could push his troops to the last hint of daylight by delaying the drum and bugle announcement and the lowering of the colors from the parade ground flagstaff. On the other hand, an easygoing officer might ease the ceremony ahead a bit and get that much of a jump on the evening's drinking.

Longarm had no idea how close to the mark Lieutenant Willis called things here, so he showed up plenty early in anticipation of his scheduled duel with Raphael deNunzio.

His point, of course, was that he wanted to get this tended to while there was still some light in the sky, which was the difficulty inherent in the choice of retreat for a starting time. It was damned difficult to have a proper duel after dark.

Longarm struck a match and applied it to the tip of his cheroot, inhaling slowly and tilting his head against the rising curl of white smoke while he peered toward the fiery red-gold sun that was sinking toward the hilltops to the west.

As soon as the last direct rays disappeared, a signal cannon boomed out and the drums began a roll. The first bell-clear tones of the bugle call drifted up from the parade ground, and Longarm nodded with satisfaction. Good. He didn't know if this timing was customary or if it had been set forward to accommodate deNunzio, but at least it left them some daylight to work with. Retreat this evening was sounding a good half hour before true sundown, the elevation of the hills west of Camp Brunot providing the difference.

Longarm grunted and stood, watching down the swale for the arrival of his people. He hoped nothing happened to detain them.

Within two or three minutes after the last bugle notes died away, Longarm could see the advance of deNunzio's party.

Predictably enough, Second Lieutenant Raphael deNunzio was done up in his finest toggery. If there'd been any sunshine to reflect off all that glitter, the man would've fair been a hazard to the eyesight of onlookers.

He wore buckles and buttons that looked as if they were real gold. And probably were. He had gold braid draped in voluminous loops and folds at his left shoulder and drooling halfway down his left side. His sword sash was made of gold braid as well, its tassels and monkey-knots of bright, bright gold falling all the way down to the tops of his brightly polished knee-high dress boots.

His spurs were polished nickel. As was a gorget that dangled on the breast of his uniform. As was the sheath for his fancy dress sword. As was, even, the tall, conical crown of a shako helmet. The shako had a little bitty gold-plated visor on it and a white cockade plume that stood at least two feet high, and there was a ducky little white leather strap that was snugged tight against deNunzio's lower lip to keep the unwieldy helmet from toppling over in a breeze.

Longarm thought he'd never seen a toy tin soldier that was got up half so cute as ol' Raphael had turned himself out for this duel.

And bright? Lordy. Catch a slant of direct sunlight and he'd look like a pillar of fire all glittery and gleamy and shining.

Longarm worked at it some and managed to keep from laughing.

He shifted his cheroot to the corner of his jaw and nodded a hello to the three men who were marching near.

There was deNunzio himself, of course. Impossible to've missed him even if a body tried. There was Sergeant Major Gompert carrying a long, thin box that was covered with green leather and had a piano hinge on the back of the lid and a line of bright brass latches down the front. The box hadn't been equipped with a handle for ease of carrying, though. Longarm thought the box looked suspiciously sized and shaped to be holding a sword or two.

The third man of this group was the post trader Roach, the one who'd mistaken Longarm for an employee of the freight company earlier. No doubt he was aware of the truth now, though.

"Gentlemen," Longarm said by way of greeting.

"Marshal." Everybody exchanged nods but not handshakes.

"I believe you have met Mr. Roach, sir," Gompert said. As deNunzio's second, he was doing the talking for the resplendent officer.

"I have had that pleasure, yes."

"Mr. Roach will serve as surgeon for the affair, sir. We, uh, have no physician assigned to Camp Brunot."

Longarm nodded to the sutler again. "I had no idea you were a doctor, too, Mr. Roach. Or should I call you—"

Roach colored slightly as Gompert cut in with the explanation. "Mr. Roach was trained as a barber-surgeon, Marshal Long. And I personally have witnessed his abilities in dealing with the regiment's wounded during the recent uprising in Colorado. No physician could have done better. If you have objection, sir, I suggest—"

"I have no objection," Longarm said quickly. "Mr. Roach's qualifications are entirely satisfactory to me." He emphasized the statement with a bow in Roach's direction.

"Thank you, sir," Gompert said. Despite the stiffness that appeared to be a part of the man's nature, Longarm thought he seemed pleased. Probably because it was plain that the deputy was going along with the rigid formalities imposed by the traditions of gentlemanly honor.

They were rather stupid formalities, in Longarm's opinion. But these guys obviously took them quite seriously, indeed. And of course they were entitled to do so.

"You choose not to be represented, sir?" Gompert asked.

"On the contrary, Sergeant Major. My party has been delayed a moment. I'm sure they will join us in no more than another minute or two."

"Very well, sir." Gompert came stiffly to attention, saluted Longarm, spun around, and saluted deNunzio, who was staring off into the distance, and then began relating the whole damned conversation to deNunzio. Like as if the guy hadn't been standing right there listening to it all the first time around. Shee-it.

Longarm coughed into his fist in an effort to hide his amusement at all this damnfoolishness. Then he turned—dutifully pretending that he couldn't hear anything Gompert was saying to deNunzio—and looked down the swale for his missing attendants.

What he found himself thinking about was what was gonna happen if Billy Vail ever got word that his top deputy'd gone and agreed to meet an army officer in a duel.

Billy was fairly loose on the subject of laws being bent now and then. But he wasn't particularly keen on his deputies shattering them.

And as far as Longarm remembered, the laws against dueling were right clear on the subject. And were federal statutes at that.

Oh, well. It all seemed necessary if he was ever gonna have a chance to sit down with Raphael deNunzio and get some straight answers.

And it damned well better be straight talk that he carried back to old Pissing Horse and the rest of the Ute.

Anything else and there'd be blood fertilizing this corner of Utah.

Gompert and deNunzio finished their conversation, and Gompert opened the leather box he was still carrying. "In case you want to inspect the weapons, sir," he said to Longarm. "Although naturally you will not be required to make your choice until your own second arrives, sir." This time he actually did smile.

Longarm stepped forward and gave a cursory glance at the contents of the box. Yup. Swords, all right. Two of them. Damned businesslike, too. No engraving, no tassels, no jewelry mounted on the hafts. Just slim, sleek, sharp-tipped steel with simple bar handguards and leather wrappings on the slightly tapered hafts. And, oh, yes, both edges of the flat blade sharpened as well as the tip. A rapier, this kind was called, if Longarm remembered right.

127

That kinda said something about deNunzio. Sportsmen who engaged in fencing as a gentleman's hobby generally used the kind of swords called épées or foils, different-shaped blades but both of them designed only for thrusting and easy to safely make blunt when the purpose of the bout was fun and not blood.

Raphael deNunzio's rapiers would cut as well as thrust. And there was no way to keep them from being deadly. Any time they were taken up, there was the likelihood of seeing blood. And maybe death as well.

Well, Longarm hadn't ever actually thought the man was funning with him.

But it was interesting that the swords confirmed it.

"You don't want to examine them?" Gompert asked.

"Naw, no point in it," Longarm said.

"I beg your pardon?"

Longarm grinned and exhaled a stream of smoke. "The way I understand it, old fellow, as the challenged party, the choice of weapons is mine. Not his."

"Well, yes, but—"

"If you'll look down the way there, you'll see that my attendants are comin' now. An' my choice o' weapons with 'em."

The gentlemen—including Lieutenant deNunzio, who wasn't supposed to be hearing any of this—turned to see Swimming Deer and Mess Sergeant Horace Rogers approaching.

Swimming Deer was pushing a handcart that was loaded with fancy picnic foods fit to serve an earl's court.

And Sergeant Rogers was carrying a pair of obsolete Springfield muskets of Civil War vintage. The .58-caliber Springfields hadn't been easy to locate this afternoon, but Rogers had been helpful in tracking some down in the enlisted men's mess. He'd explained that most regiments liked to keep some of the old muzzle loaders on hand for the purpose of hunting. The men enjoyed the hunting, and it helped give some variety to the mess menus. The muskets were preferred over cartridge arms for that purpose because a man could load them with loose shot to bring down upland game or waterfowl, then turn right around and drop a ball in for shooting deer or elk.

That information had fitted right in with what Longarm'd had in mind.

In fact, it was considerably better for his purposes than what he'd thought he would have to do.

"Muskets?" Gompert sounded quite genuinely offended.

Longarm chuckled. "Yeah, well, I didn' reckon a walkdown with Colt sixguns'd be quite fair, Sergeant Major." The chuckle died away and so did the smile that had gone with it. "No more fair, say, than rapiers woulda been."

Gompert flushed a little at that verbal shot. And so he should have, the way Longarm saw it. Shit, who'd they think they were kidding. A man who carried cased rapiers around with him—and who fought left-handed at that, which even most swordsmen might never have faced before—wasn't exactly making no sporting proposition when he suggested a duel.

The swords would've given deNunzio just about the same advantage that Longarm could quite legitimately claim by turning this "gentlemanly" duel into a quick-draw gunfight.

But then, maybe a hayseed deputy wasn't supposed to know about such things as who had the choice of weapons, hmm?

Longarm gave Gompert and deNunzio a smug look and then waited for his own entourage to reach the field of honor with the weapons and the goodies.

Chapter 29

"What'd you bring us for the victory celebration, Sergeant Rogers?" Longarm asked. He stood over the cart rubbing his hands together and eyeing the goodies that lay there nested inside a heap of puffy white linen. The other men, quite naturally, inspected the fancy foodstuffs, also.

"Cherries Jubilee," Rogers said proudly. "I'll flambé them as soon as you gentlemen have your duel done. Also some finger sandwiches, sir. A few sweetmeats. Watermelon rind pickle there. And of course the brandy. Everything as you requested, sir."

"Sounds mighty fine t' me, Sergeant. I thank you."

"Have we come here to settle a question of honor or to have a party?" Gompert complained.

"Why, I just thought it'd be nice to have a party after," Longarm said. "Those of us as is alive, that is." He chuckled and motioned Rogers forward with the pair of old-fashioned muskets. "Sergeant Major Gompert, I believe the selection of weapons is yours. Both of them are charged and loaded. I oversaw the loading myself."

Gompert grunted. The sergeant major looked at deNunzio and got a shrug in return. It was plain that Springfield muskets for the dueling weapons weren't to their liking. But the rules of the deadly game made it equally plain that they had no choice about it. The challenged party is afforded that decision, and the only refusal open to deNunzio as the challenger would be to apologize to Longarm and withdraw from the combat. Longarm really didn't figure Raphael deNunzio would be the kind to back off from something that easy. Although with powder instead of steel being used, he doubted the officer was so keen to fight as he had been when he

130

first arrived. One good push might be enough to change his mind now.

The challenger's second grimaced and gave each Springfield a brief visual inspection. The old guns were identical, give or take the dings and dents and surface scratches they'd suffered over the years.

"This one," he said, his tone of voice adding that it really didn't matter.

"Very good, Sergeant Major." Rogers handed over the musket Gompert wanted, then extended the other to Longarm.

"Thank you, Sergeant."

"My pleasure, sir." Rogers winked at Longarm, then snapped to attention and saluted him before stepping back out of the way. He joined Swimming Deer beside the cart and began fussing with plates and silverware and the soft white napery that would be used for the party.

Sergeant Major Gompert gave the other musket to deNunzio, stepped a pace backward, and saluted the gentleman smartly. "Sir! At your command, sir."

"Very well, Sergeant Major. You may see to the positioning. And be good enough to count off the commands for us as well, if you please."

"Yes, sir." Gompert whirled, saluted, and said, "Would that meet with your approval, Marshal Long?"

"It would, Sergeant Major Gompert."

"Very good, sir. Gentlemen, if you please. Lieutenant deNunzio here, facing north. Marshal Long here, facing south. That's good. Half a step to your left, Marshal? Thank you, sir. You may both stand at ease, gentlemen. Port arms, if you please. Thank you.

"Now, gentlemen, I will give the commands as follows. You will each pace forward one step at a time. I will count off the paces to the number of ten. At that time, gentlemen, you will halt and stand in place. I will ask you to arm your firelocks. At that time and not before you may draw your hammers from half to full cock, sirs. I will give you ample warning, sirs, then give you permission to fire. At that time you may at your own speed and discretion turn, aim, and fire.

131

"If a piece fails to discharge, sirs, the possessor of that weapon is entitled to another percussion cap and a second attempt to secure the discharge but only after the other party has had his opportunity to fire. If both parties fire but fail to draw blood, I will ask your pleasure. A decision by either party to continue the contest for a second round will be binding on both. Is that agreeable with you, Marshal Long? Lieutenant deNunzio? Thank you, gentlemen. Have you any questions? No? Very well, gentlemen, prepare yourselves, please. And may God be with you." Gompert barked the instructions as if he were on the parade ground drilling troops.

Longarm hawked once and spat. He was wanting a smoke. And a drink wouldn't hurt his feelings any, either. Behind him he could neither hear nor sense any hint of movement in deNunzio. The lieutenant might've been a cigar store wooden Indian for all the fidgeting he was doing. But then, he was likely an old hand at this dueling business. The kind of dueling Longarm was familiar with wasn't so nicey-nice as this, and the only rule involved was to be alive when the thing was done with. Longarm spat again.

"Forward please, gentlemen, on my command now. One . . . two . . . three . . ." The sergeant major counted them slowly forward for ten paces. "Halt please, gentlemen. Stand at rest."

Longarm sure was wanting that cheroot. Soon.

"Cock your pieces, please, gentlemen. Cock your pieces."

Longarm eared back on the big hammer. It clicked into place.

"Lieutenant deNunzio, sir. Are you ready?"

"I am." The voice sounded much more distant than twenty paces behind, but of course it was not.

"Marshal Long, sir. Are you ready?"

"All set, thank you."

"Very well. Gentlemen, on my command you may turn, aim, and fire at will. Ready about? Now!"

Longarm took his time turning. DeNunzio had already whirled and had his musket shouldered and aimed. Longarm found himself staring straight into the black maw that was the open, gaping muzzle of the old Springfield.

Funny how deNunzio's getup had seemed so silly just a few minutes ago and now didn't look the least lick silly.

Longarm braced himself, not entirely sure what to expect at this point.

He saw the circular puff of smoke blossom at the Springfield's muzzle, pale fire behind it, and a small dark mass in the center.

Longarm's eyes involuntarily closed, and he rocked a step backward at the impact that struck him low on the right side of his belly and turned him half around.

He looked down and saw a bright red mass oozing off the flat of his stomach and beginning to run onto his hip and upper thigh.

He grunted, braced himself, and raised his own musket to his shoulder.

This time he was the one peering over the steel sights. His hand was steady, and he knew his aim would be, too.

"Jesus!" deNunzio blurted.

Longarm looked into deNunzio's eyes. Then away. Lower. Deliberately slow and obvious about it. Dropped his point of aim from the spot between Raphael deNunzio's eyes down to his chest. To his stomach. Finally came to rest with his aim resting squarely on the tip of the vee formed by the man's crotch. A lead ball slicing into flesh at that point . . .

"No. Please." DeNunzio spun, presenting his back to Longarm. "Not . . . shoot me, damn you, but not there. Not there. Jesus, not there." The man dropped to his knees and began to tremble.

Longarm grunted and fired his musket into the ground beside deNunzio's left knee.

The shot created a helluv an ugly wound on the soil there. Red gore and everything.

"What the . . . ?"

Longarm snickered and wiped at the "blood" on his side with a fingertip. He lifted it to his mouth and sucked the gooey red stuff off his finger.

"Not bad," he said. "But it rightly needs t' be flambéed, Sergeant. Just like you said it oughta."

"What the hell have you done?" Gompert bellowed.

"Ask your boy deNunzio there, Sergeant Major. He's the one down on his knees." Longarm tossed his musket to Rogers and got a wink in return. "Make sure your kitchen help washes

133

these guns out real good, Sergeant. If the sauce them cherries are in is allowed t' dry inside the bores, these guns won't be worth nothin', you know."

"I'll see to it, sir."

"Reckon you can light off the flambé now, Sergeant. An' Lieutenant deNunzio, let's you and me have a talk quick as we have ourselves a bite t' eat. Couple things I want t' know from you. Starting with why in hell you and me been having us this duel t' begin with."

Swimming Deer began passing refreshments around just about the time the last good light was fading from the sky.

If nothing else, Longarm figured, the Ute tribe would know about this so-called duel before the dawning. That was the reason he'd wanted her along.

"Are you all right, Sergeant Major? You look a mite confused. Have a taste o' this brandy. It'll put some lead in your pencil." Longarm pressed a glass of the stuff into Gompert's hands and turned to see what he could do for Roach next.

Far as duels went, he figured, this'un hadn't been all bad.

Chapter 30

Raphael deNunzio acted subdued and slightly out of touch with reality. No wonder, Longarm thought. The man had just been shaken to his roots. He'd had a duelist's proud, macho image of himself, and Longarm had shattered it—or at the very least put a helluva dent into it—with that ungentlemanly aiming point that threatened the poor bastard's nuts. Given a choice between death and cowardice, a man like Lieutenant deNunzio would never hesitate to stand tall and pick death over dishonor. But when the choice was to publicly cringe or let himself be neutered . . . there just weren't very many folks idiot enough to let some other S.O.B. turn 'em into a eunuch. Raphael deNunzio's big problem was that he couldn't see the lunacy that was inherent in those choices.

"Another glass o' brandy, Raphael?" Longarm asked, sidling over beside the officer and taking his elbow in a gesture meant to encourage friendly confidence.

"No, thank you."

"How,'bout another bite t' eat, then?"

"No, I'm . . . all right now. Thank you."

Longarm glanced at the others, who seemed pretty much preoccupied with the picnic comestibles. "C'mon over here a minute, Raphael. There's some things I think you and me should talk about."

The lieutenant allowed himself to be led out of hearing from the others. Longarm chose a likely-looking slab of rock and got them both seated on it.

"Why?" he asked.

DeNunzio peered not at Longarm but at his own nervously twisting hands. "Why what?"

"Don't bullshit me, Raphael. You know what I'm asking.

You oughta know, too, that whatever you say t' me will stay right here. I mean, I might have t' put some of it into an official report. But won't none of it be gassed around Camp Brunot and won't none of it be whispered along t' the army. No matter what it is."

"I . . . love her."

"Shit, you don't hafta sound so miserable when you say that, do you? It strikes me that that oughta be a happy thing for a fella t' be able to say."

"I've dishonored myself. And her."

"Bullshit."

"You saw how I acted."

"What I seen, Raphael, was that you stayed where you was. You never tried to run away. You thought I was shot half in two and was wanting revenge, but you never took so much as a step away from my musket."

"I turned away from your aim, sir. I dishonored myself and by implication dishonored as well the most lovely, the most delicate, the most gentle and dear woman I have ever—"

"Raphael, will you quit hittin' yourself over the head with your own imagination? You never dishonored nobody today. You covered your balls and stood right there so's I could kill you if that was what I wanted. There's no fault in that."

"I dispute you, sir. I was in the wrong today. And for that I apologize. If there is any way I can make amends . . ."

"Fact is, Raphael, there is a way. Which is to answer my questions. That's the satisfaction I'd want. Then we'll call 'er square and be done with it."

DeNunzio swallowed. It took him a moment of discomfort to think things through. Then he nodded. "What do you want to know, Long?"

"First thing, dammit, I want t' know why you an' me was fighting out here this evening. What'd I ever do t' make you hate me?"

"Why, I certainly do not hate you, Long. Far from it. I . . . would admit to a certain amount of jealousy. But hate? Not at all."

"Then why'd we go an' have us a duel, Raphael?"

"Because you offended Clytemnestra, Long. You broke a promise to her and made her angry. You hurt her feelings.

136

I could not allow that to go unanswered, sir." The tone of deNunzio's voice changed when he got into that. He'd found his backbone again, at least so far as the widow Benhurst was concerned.

"Broke a promise?"

"She was distressed about it, too. I happened by last night, you see. To ask if there was anything she needed. I found her in tears. You had promised to take supper with her. But you failed to appear, didn't even send a note of apology. She was devastated. And I must admit to feelings of jealousy because she was so distraught over your behavior. I assumed, and still do, that she had been powerfully attracted to you. Then, when I found her like that, actually weeping . . . I tried to comfort her as best I was able. One thing led to another. To an awakening, if you will. And I . . . last night, sometime this morning . . . I found myself in love with Mrs. Benhurst. Can you imagine it?"

DeNunzio shook his head as if in wonder. "I have broken more hearts than you can imagine, Long. No, don't look at me like that. It is true. Why do you think I've remained so junior an officer when others all around me have secured promotion? Jealousy, sir. Whisper and rumor and jealousy. My commanders have always been nervous about their wives when I have been in their command. And I daresay they had good reason. That is why I am today only a second lieutenant and why I find myself in this godforsaken country now. Jealousy on the part of others. But always before, sir, I've enjoyed the dalliances and never gave a thought to the broken hearts I may have left behind me. But now . . . now I am the one who is trapped in the pain of true love, sir. I am the one who has fallen deeply and truly in love with Clytemnestra." He shrugged. "How else could I have responded, sir, when I was confronted by the man who so offended her?"

Longarm grunted and lighted a cheroot. "Saying thank you comes t' mind. Since I was the one brought you two t'gether, so t' speak."

"You are making a joke now"—deNunzio blinked—"aren't you?"

"Well, fact is, I was busy last night an' plumb forgot I'd said I'd take supper with the lady. Next time I see her I'll try an' remember t' say I'm sorry."

"I would prefer that you not see her again, sir," deNunzio said stiffly.

Longarm puffed on his cigar and decided there was no point in debating the man on that subject. If there was any need for him to talk to Sly Benhurst again, he would damn sure do it. If there wasn't, well, he didn't much care either way. But then, he wasn't the one who was smitten heart and soul by the pretty little widow woman.

"You've answered me 'bout the reason for our fight," Longarm said, "and I thank you. Something else I need t' know though, Raphael."

"And that would be?"

"Did you kill Bird Talks to the Moon this morning?"

DeNunzio snapped bolt upright on the rock where he was sitting. "Sir?"

"Don't put on that insulted act, dammit. An' before you open your mouth again, which I can see you achin' t' do there, I want you t' know: you throw another challenge at me, buddy boy, I won't take it so light a second time. You listening? Good. If you want t' challenge me to a duel a second time, mister, I'll meet you face to face with holstered revolvers an' standing six foot apart. Believe me, Raphael, if it comes to that kinda duel, I'd be able t' clip your buttons off an' drop your britches around your ankles before you ever got a gun clear o' leather. I ain't trying to brag about that. Just stating a fact."

Raphael deNunzio thought better of whatever it was he had been about to say.

"Now, what I asked you, Raphael, is did you or did you not kill a Ute Indian named Bird Talks to the Moon this morning?"

"I did not," deNunzio declared with considerable heat.

"He's alive?"

"He is."

"Be all right if I verify that?"

"Why should you, Long? That Indian has nothing to do with you."

"I agree that he don't," Longarm said. "I come here looking for a wanted man. Next thing I know a Ute that I'm acquainted with—old Pissing Horse, if it matters—has me in his lodge t'

138

talk over old times. Then this morning while I'm trying to have my breakfast, there's this big stir and the Ute are fixing t' go to war because they believe some Ute named Bird Talks has been beat to death by a certain lieutenant here at Camp Brunot. Is any o' this commencing t' sound familiar, Raphael?"

"Bird Talks to the Moon is alive and well, Long. Did the Ute really threaten warfare?"

"Hell, I wouldn't call it a threat. What it is, man, is a promise. They want t' know that their kinsman is all right. An' the truth is, I told 'em I'd come in an' find out for them. Which is what I'm trying to do with you right now."

"I see." DeNunzio gnawed at his lower lip. "You wouldn't happen to have one of those cigars to spare, would you? I've left mine back at my quarters."

Longarm passed one to him and let the officer take his time—time he no doubt used so he could collect his thoughts—about trimming and lighting it.

"Thanks." DeNunzio leaned back and blew a stream of pale smoke into the air. "Where were we, Long?"

"You know damn good an' well where we were. Now, get on with it, if you please."

Chapter 31

"I did not 'beat' Bird Talks to the Moon, Longarm. I . . . disciplined him," deNunzio said.

"Disciplined," Longarm repeated cautiously.

"That's right. It was nothing more severe than that."

"You took him out o' the guard tent, had him tied spread eagle, an' . . . 'disciplined' him?"

DeNunzio gave him a worried look.

"What, I wasn't supposed to know you had him tied down so you could beat him easier? Sorry, but that ain't much of a secret. The Ute told it to me."

"Bird Talks to the Moon is a scout, officially enrolled as an employee of the United States Army, I might add, and as such he is subject to all the rules of discipline—"

"Dammit, Raphael, you ain't dealing with some ignorant savage here. Not when you talk t' me nor for that matter when you talk t' old Pissing Horse. That old fart looks like a louse-ridden, half-wit blanket Injun, I know, but he's about as easy to blow smoke over as a riverboat gambler would be, Raphael. An' that's something you army boys oughta figure out for your own damned peace o' mind. I happen t' know that Pissing Horse has already hired a mighty smart civilian lawyer t' look into this thing with Bird Talks to the Moon. And all you're doing with your so-called discipline is giving that lawyer ammunition to put your tit in a wringer, Lieutenant. So quit trying t' confuse things an' start telling me some straight shit here. Maybe it ain't occurred to you yet, man, but I'm the one neutral party there is around here. Give me some help so's I can maybe grease the skids an' make things slide along better for everybody."

DeNunzio shifted uncomfortably on the rock slab he was

140

sitting on. "All right, dammit. All right." He sighed loudly. "I've already told you what happened between Clytemnestra and me last night. It was . . . beautiful. But then this morning I . . . couldn't get it out of my mind. The things that vile buck did to her, I mean. When she was his captive, you see. You may not know about that, Long. But the Indian Bird Talks to the Moon is the one who murdered Major Benhurst and the enlisted escorts. He took Clytemnestra captive and . . . ravaged her. Against her will, naturally. He forced himself upon her. I . . . couldn't bear to think of that—but I couldn't make myself *stop* thinking about it. It tore at me and gave me no peace. And this morning . . . you could say that I snapped. I had the guards bring the Indian out for questioning. Had them tie him to a wagon wheel. And before you begin quoting law to me, I am quite well aware that spread-eagling is no longer an authorized form of punishment with or without court-martial. I had Bird Talks tied nonetheless, sir. And I proceeded to exact some small measure of revenge for what that man did to my beloved Clytemnestra. And no matter what you may say or think, sir, I will *not* consent to apologize for my actions. Not to you and certainly not to those Indians. I would do any or every part of it all over again, in fact. Probably I should have killed the man this morning when I could. I . . . indeed, I did try. I admit that, sir. I did my level best to beat that bastard to death. One of the enlisted men stopped me. I've wished ever since that he hadn't. I really do believe it would have been better if I had killed the vile savage then and there."

"The army'd be at war with the whole Ute nation if you had, Raphael."

"If that would prevent some other innocent women from coming to the same harm that dear Clytemnestra suffered, then I say it would be a small price for the benefit."

"And if Mrs. Benhurst was one o' those who was killed before it was over, Raphael? How would you view it then?"

"She wouldn't be. I would see to that, sir. I would defend her with my life. I would give her my all. In fact, sir, if she will have me, I intend to do precisely that. And no simple-minded savages could bring her to harm now that she is under my protection." DeNunzio's jaw was set and his eyes were squinting about half shut and he was past all reason.

At least on that subject. Longarm could read the signs clear as handwriting on clean paper. Never mind the fact that the soldiers at Camp Brunot were few in number and were totally unprepared for a fight. Never mind that if they went to war, the Ute would be coming in hard and fast and completely by surprise. Never mind reality. To officers like Raphael deNunzio, especially at times when their emotions were aroused, there simply wasn't any such thing as a bunch of naked, howling savages who could possibly stand up to the innate superiority of the white race.

Yeah. Right. Just ask a major named Dade. Or more recently that fella called Fetterman. Or most recent of all the dashing and glamorous Custer.

Any of those three could've testified about the fighting ability of Indian opponents.

"But you didn't kill him," Longarm said, trying to bring the conversation back to something approaching reality.

"I did not."

"You did beat him."

"I did."

Longarm grunted and drew smoke from his cheroot deep into his lungs, holding it there a moment before he exhaled again.

The truth, of course, was that he could understand perfectly well what Raphael deNunzio had been feeling this morning.

Longarm had felt something quite similar himself just yesterday, he recalled. And that was without being in love with the widow Benhurst. All he'd done was listen to the lady give a brief account of her kidnaping. There had been no details offered about the indignities committed upon her person by Bird Talks to the Moon. Nor should there have been. Yet even so Longarm had found himself welling up with rage at the Indian. Had himself felt impelled toward punishing the man. If Clytemnestra Benhurst's story had affected Longarm like that, how much more powerful must it have been on a man who was in love with her?

"I'll need to see for myself that Bird Talks to the Moon is alive and well, Raphael. I'll see him and then report back to Pissing Horse. Pissing Horse will take my word that Bird Talks is all right. There won't be a war. And I won't bother

142

you no more about Bird Talks to the Moon. This will put an end to it, I promise."

Raphael deNunzio grimaced and cleared his throat loudly. He stared off into the newly fallen night for a moment. Then he shook his head.

"I'm sorry, Marshal. I can't let you do that."

Chapter 32

"This don't make no sense, Raphael. You know that, don't you?"

DeNunzio shrugged and looked away.

"Damn you, I'm trying to stop a war from happening. Don't you understand that?"

"It isn't my choice to make, Long."

"Bullshit."

"It is beyond my control. Or yours."

"I'm not asking that you release the bastard, dammit. I just want t' talk to him. See that he's alive. Jesus, man, that ain't nothing. I don't want him out o' custody any more'n you do. Far as I'm concerned, after what he done, ol' Bird Talks to the Moon can rot till the moon talks back to him. But I can't allow your damnfoolishness to let a war get started, mister. I got to see that that Indian is alive. An' it wouldn't hurt none if I could get your promise that he won't be beat on like that again."

DeNunzio swallowed. Hard. "If it helps, Long, I can give you my word that I'll not discipline the detainee again. But that is as far as I am able to go. You may not speak with him; you may not see him. No one can."

"You ain't making sense."

The officer exhaled, twin streams of smoke jetting from his nostrils. He was refusing to look at Longarm now.

And no wonder, Longarm figured. The S.O.B. was being completely unreasonable here. There just wasn't any valid reason why a federal officer shouldn't be allowed to view the prisoner. Or detainee. Whatever the fuck they wanted to call him at this point.

"Are you gonna tell me why you're acting like this?" Longarm asked.

DeNunzio pretended that he hadn't heard.

"Mister, with or without your permission, I am *going* to have my look at Bird Talks to the Moon."

"The guards have orders to shoot."

"I don't think there's a soldier on this post . . . 'cept that hard-nosed Gompert, maybe . . . who's cold enough t' shoot down a United States marshal. Not out in the open an' with time enough to think an' talk about it, they wouldn't."

"I would," deNunzio said.

"Shoot down a man who's no threat to you, Raphael? I don't think so. The kind o' man who still believes in a code o' honor wouldn't do no such."

"I would, Long. I swear to you. If you approach the guard tent, I will shoot you myself."

"Why?" Longarm persisted.

DeNunzio only shook his head again. The man looked thoroughly miserable now. But he wasn't backing away from his declaration. If it came to that, he would shoot. Or so he said.

"I reckon you got to do what you see as best," Longarm said unhappily. "An' me, Raphael, I got t' do the same. An' the thing I see that needs doing the most is stopping these Ute from going to war. You understand that? It's more important than whatever is gnawing on you about one shit-for-brains murdering Indian like Bird Talks to the Moon. No matter *what*."

The lieutenant was trembling now. He looked near to the end of his rope. Yet even so he would not relent. He only hunched his shoulders and peered off toward the horizon, misery reflecting moist and empty in his eyes.

The hell with it. Longarm stood, paused for a moment, but found no parting words that he thought might somehow help change deNunzio's mind, and finally turned and walked quietly away.

Chapter 33

Longarm sat next to Swimming Deer on a cot in the storage tent near the officers' mess kitchen. The other Ute serving girls were nowhere around. Nor for that matter was Mess Sergeant Rogers.

Longarm had no idea where the Indian girls were this evening, but he had a pretty good idea that Rogers wouldn't be around to overhear his conversation with Swimming Deer. Not for a good many hours.

By way of a thank-you for the mess sergeant's help earlier, Longarm had set the man up to a blowout at the sutler's store. At Longarm's expense. And while he'd been at it, he'd extended the invitation to any of Joey Dunfrey's teamsters who were still around and to the transportation sergeant Hendricks, too.

Clytemnestra Benhurst's angry reaction about him not showing up for supper reminded Longarm that he'd been passing out promises pretty heavy ever since he got to Brunot but hadn't been making good on them worth a damn. It was time he changed that lest bad habits set in and he let himself become a liar about such petty little details. A man's reputation, after all, is a fragile thing that needs—and is worth—tending.

A side benefit to paying off those obligations tonight was that he had some privacy with Swimming Deer now. His own VOQ tent was apt to be watched if deNunzio truly intended to keep him from seeing Bird Talks to the Moon.

Not that Longarm knew what he was gonna do next. Not hardly.

He sighed and tried to ignore the warm and teasing hand that Swimming Deer had placed in his lap.

"Later, pretty girl," he said.

"Promise?"

"Sure." There. He'd gone and done it again. Another promise that would have to be fulfilled no matter how casually it'd been given. Well, it wasn't like this one would be such a burden to have to pay off. Wasn't like he was gonna forget about it, either. He smiled and kissed her on the cheek and resolutely removed her hand from his lap. The girl pouted a little but didn't complain.

"Tell me, Swimming Deer, is there any way I could sneak in an' see Bird Talks?"

She shook her head. "One guard outside. Pah. Sneak easy like a shadow, he never know. But guard inside, down in hole with Bird Talk, he know. Hear everything. See everything. Shoot, oh, yes. That guard, no place to go around. He is there with Bird Talk. Always awake. Ready to shoot. You don't go there, Long Long."

"No, I suppose not," Longarm reluctantly agreed. He pulled out a cheroot and lighted it, musing silently to himself while his hands were occupied with the familiar tasks of manipulating cigar and match.

"Has anyone tried to talk to him?" he asked.

"Oh, yes. When Bird Talk first put in hole. Try and try, but no good, Long Long. No one can get near, eh?"

"Would you mind telling me who it was that made the attempt, Swimming Deer?"

"Why?"

"I want to talk to him. Or her. I want to see if there's anything they saw that might help me find a chink in the armor."

"Armor, Long Long? What is armor?"

"Never mind armor, Swimming Deer. Just let me talk to whoever has tried to get into that guard tent."

She thought that over for a moment, then sighed. "Hokay." She stood and took him by the hand. "Come, Long Long."

Longarm could've kicked himself for not thinking about coming here himself. Hell, it only stood to reason. Bird Talks to the Moon was an enrolled scout serving in a completely official capacity as an employee of the U.S. Army. Well, where there was one scout, there would be others. Longarm should've thought to go looking for those other Indians. After all, who would know Bird Talks better than the other scouts?

And who would be more anxious to know that he was all right in captivity?

The scouts' camp was set up well apart from the main post, a ridge of shale separating it from the Camp Brunot grounds, probably to keep the Indian encampment from becoming, by army standards, an eyesore.

Not that there was anything ugly about it. Semipermanent arbors had been erected and coup poles placed in front of them. Longarm thought it a right tidy arrangement even if things did kinda meander and sprawl. On the other hand, an army officer accustomed to having everything laid out in straight lines and logical order would probably wince every time he had to look at the untrammeled individualism the Ute displayed in their quarters here.

For some reason Swimming Deer led him to the scout camp on a straight line. That might be the shortest route, but it damn sure wasn't the easiest because it meant climbing up the shale ridge and then slithering and clattering down the other side. Longarm thought it would've been easier if they'd walked around to the end of the ridgeline. It wasn't all that far, if he remembered correctly.

Still, he wasn't bitching. If the girl wanted to climb a little, why not?

They descended the far slope amid a shower of loose shale chips dislodged by their passage and walked to a fire ring placed more or less in the center of things. At the moment there was no fire blazing, but a number of Ute warriors were hunkered in a circle around the coals of what must have been their supper fire.

"H'lo, Arm Long," one of the dark, dimly seen figures said.

"You know me?"

"I do."

"It is dark, friend, and your voice is not familiar to me. Do I know you?"

"I am Jimmy Weak Dog, son of Two Feathers."

"I remember you, Jimmy Weak Dog. Are your parents well?"

"They are at the old reservation in Colorado, Arm Long. They are well for now. My father will die in the winter to come."

"I'm sorry to hear that, Jimmy." Longarm carefully did not contradict the young man's belief. If Jimmy believed it—or more to the point, if Two Feathers himself believed it—then it would become so. The old man would die sometime during this next winter.

Jimmy Weak Dog grunted. "I will tell them you asked about them. But that is not why you came here."

"No, it is not."

"Eat with us, Arm Long. Woman, see to this man's food. Then we will talk. We will tell you whatever you wan' to know, Arm Long. We will be friends together."

There was a slight stirring among the half dozen or so men around the circle, and a girl—Longarm remembered her as one of the girls who served in the officers' mess at Camp Brunot—came forward to pile dried grass and twigs on the coals and build the fire up again. While she was doing that, Swimming Deer ghosted away into the night to get the food Jimmy Weak Dog demanded. It was pretty plain that Jimmy Weak Dog was the boss here. Whether the army knew it or not.

Longarm threw his head back. Laughed loudly. Thumped his thigh in appreciation of the hilarious tale Jimmy Weak Dog was telling.

All around them the other scouts were chanting a song as loudly as they could sing it. Judging from the giggling the girls were doing, the song was about as bawdy as it was loud. Since it was sung in the Ute language, though, Longarm had to assume that without knowing it for sure.

Oh, they were having a wonderful time here, they were. Everybody gay and friendly.

And loud.

Longarm smiled and bobbed his head and smiled some more.

He accepted another chunk of meat wrapped in pan bread, belched and grinned. "Thanks."

"Eat, Arm Long? Drink, too? We have whiskey. Good whiskey. Many bottle."

"No, thanks, no whiskey." This didn't seem the right time to be getting into questions about the legality of Jimmy Weak Dog and his scouts possessing whiskey. " 'Scuse me, Jimmy.

149

Gotta take a leak now." Longarm stood, laughed a little, ambled idly away from the fire toward the shadows.

He was the very picture of the "hale fellow well met," all happy and loose and just having a nice ol' time with a bunch of good friends.

But once the singing, carousing, shouting Ute were behind him and he was alone in the night, the smile melted off his face, and his lanky wandering gait was transformed into the sure and deliberate movements of a nocturnal predator that scents prey and has begun its stalk.

His expression then was coldly suspicious, and his eyes shifted and assessed every shadow, every motion. He moved forward through the night like a silent wraith.

Chapter 34

Whyn't you try teaching your grandmother t' suck eggs, Jimmy m' boy, Longarm silently suggested.

Because this other shit sure as hell hadn't worked.

Huh. It was practically insulting, the youngster thinking he could put something over on Arm Long that easy.

Why, just how stupid did they think Longarm was, anyhow? Shee-it. They were gonna have to weave a tighter cloth than this if they were gonna pull the wool over his eyes an' hope to get away with it.

He'd been suspicious enough when Swimming Deer took him over difficult and potentially dangerous loose shale at night. Ground like that was practically built for falling on, and she would know it. But it sure made a racket when those chips rained down the hillside. Going up and over the ridge had alerted the camp to their coming long before they were close enough to see anything. The scouts had had plenty of time to assemble innocently at the circle.

And then all that loud singing and bullshit? Right. Pissing Horse's band fixing to go to war, but Jimmy Weak Dog isn't supposed to know about it? Or if he did know isn't supposed to be wary of white visitors? Why, we'll all just gather round and have us a party anyhow, right? And a loud one at that. Shee-double-it.

These scouts and the Ute girls who worked at Brunot were up to something. Furthermore, whatever it was made noise. Which they'd tried to cover over.

Except it wasn't all that easy to fool an old he-coon like Arm Long.

He'd heard the grunting and thumping twenty, thirty minutes ago. Followed by the appearance at the fire circle of another

151

two sweaty and winded young men with girls on their arms.

Maybe Longarm was supposed to believe that the fellows had gotten sweaty from being off in the bushes with the girls. Except somebody should've remembered to get the girls to breathing heavy, too. They hadn't been.

As it was, well, he'd caught enough hints of sound to figure out the direction he needed to go. That should be more than enough to guide him.

He walked well out of sight from the fire ring, then dropped into a crouch and circled wide around.

The arbors that housed the army scouts were low, loaf-shaped black lumps that were faintly visible against the charcoal gray of the night. Moonlight would have helped, but the quarter moon hadn't cleared the horizon yet.

Longarm didn't know what he was looking for, but he was positive this was the place he needed to be looking in. He'd heard enough noise to tell him that much.

He stopped. Swiveled. Frowned.

Those low, lumpy arbors just in front of him. There was something about them, something vaguely . . . different.

Then he realized. Hell, yes. All the other low-to-the-ground shapes were softly rounded. These looked quite square and regular in shape.

He moved toward them and knelt. Reached out and lightly touched the nearest one.

"Shit," he said out loud.

Crates. Wooden crates like were piled all over the grounds at Camp Brunot.

Except the peculiar size and shape of these particular crates meant that he didn't really have to open one to see what they contained.

The scouts were busy raiding the unguarded army supplies for rifles and ammunition, dammit.

This right here was the reason Pissing Horse was willing to delay going to war. The old fox was giving his boys—whose loyalty lay more with clan and tribe than it did with the soldiers in blue—time enough to steal the wherewithal for the warfare.

Longarm stood. The cartilage in his knee joints popped, the sound of it seeming unnaturally loud.

"I am sad, Arm Long. It would be better if you laugh and drink with us. Now you see things you should not see. Now what we must to do with you, eh?"

There were four, maybe five of them. Or possibly more than that. Longarm could only see the four for sure and a shadow that might have been a fifth warrior.

Jimmy Weak Dog and his boys couldn't fool Arm Long, and they couldn't carry crates of rifles in the dark without making a little noise.

But they could sneak up on a fella just fine once they set their minds to it.

Longarm looked at them. And didn't like his chances.

Working for him was the fact that the Ute scouts were all armed with old Springfield rifles that'd been cut down to carbine length and given an Allyn trapdoor conversion so they would breech-load standard army cartridges. Those cheap, makeshift carbines were sturdy as hell and approximately as dependable as rocks. But they were single-shot weapons and slow to reload. In a firefight Longarm and his Colt would have all the advantage.

If, that is, he lived past the first furious flurry.

Working against him, dammit, was that he knew for sure where only four of the scouts were and suspected the location of a fifth.

But that wasn't all of them. And he had no idea if the missing Indians were still squatting beside the fire or if they were ten feet away from him with carbines in their hands and a willingness to take his scalp if that was what things came down to.

Not knowing how many Ute were in front of him or where they all were, it would be out and out suicide for him to drag iron on them now. Longarm was sure of that.

One other thing he did know for certain sure. And that was that if push came to shove, these boys would kill him as quick as they would any other man.

Never mind that Arm Long was known to be a friend of the Ute tribe. Never mind that as of tonight they weren't at war with anybody.

The blunt fact was that if squat came to shit, they would raise his hair and never look back.

153

Longarm had no illusions about that.

"I came here to talk, Jimmy Weak Dog. I have kept no secrets from you. Now you have no secrets from me. This is good. Now we can sit in the fire circle and talk as one man to another, you and me. Or would you dishonor your people and shoot me, instead? Pissing Horse gave me three days, Jimmy Weak Dog. Only one day has passed. Would you shoot me now? If you do, Jimmy Weak Dog, you must shoot me as a coward shoots. You must shoot me in the back."

Longarm turned away and began walking back to the council fire.

There was a tiny spot of intense heat concentrated high on his back, just about midway between his shoulder blades. If any one of the Ute scouts fired at him, he figured, that should be about where the bullet would go.

Longarm focused his attention on keeping his gait loose and his manner easy as he strolled back toward the circle.

It was out of his hands now. If any of them decided to shoot . . .

Chapter 35

The warriors filed back to the circle and resumed their seats. This time, though, there was no pretense of laughter and gaiety. This time their expressions were as serious as the situation demanded.

"Has our brother been murdered, Arm Long? Must we fight to avenge Bird Talks to Moon?" Jimmy Weak Dog's voice was soft and because of that seemed all the more serious and menacing.

Longarm took his time looking over the leader of the scouts and then each of the other young warriors in turn.

They were an impressive bunch, he conceded. Lean and brave. Ready to fight. Ready if need be to die as well.

They wore white man's clothing and carried white man's weapons. They were Ute warriors beneath those unimportant trappings, and they were proud.

"I have not seen your brother," Longarm told them. "Lieutenant deNunzio assures me that Bird Talks is alive. Lieutenant deNunzio gave me his word as an officer and a gentleman that no one ever again will be allowed to do to Bird Talks what Lieutenant deNunzio did to him this morning. Lieutenant deNunzio said to me that he was angry with Bird Talks this morning. Lieutenant deNunzio has fallen in love with the widow of the old major, the lady Bird Talks kidnapped and raped after he murdered her husband. Lieutenant deNunzio thought about Bird Talks rutting on this woman who Lieutenant deNunzio loves, and he wanted to punish Bird Talks for this. Think on this, Jimmy Weak Dog. You are a man. You would want to do no less to any man who forced himself on your woman. That is why Lieutenant deNunzio did this morning what he did. Now Lieutenant deNunzio is ashamed, but now it is too late to call back what was already done." That was gilding the lily and then some, but Longarm figured it was close to the truth. So close that it wasn't enough of a lie to count against him. Hell, if deNunzio wasn't ashamed of himself, he oughta be.

"You have seen for yourself that Bird Talks to Moon is well?"

"I have not," Longarm repeated. "This was told to me by Lieutenant deNunzio. He gave his word on it."

"The word of Nunzie is no more to me than the word of Two Face Woman, Arm Long. I do not want his word. Pissing Horse does not want his word. Want *your* word."

Longarm groaned. He wasn't out of the woods yet, even if they were sitting and talking with him. The scouts' Springfield carbines were still across their knees. Their knives rested in beaded sheaths at their waists. Yet in no more than an eyeblink of time this seemingly peaceful assemblage of young men could burst forth in bloodlust, shooting and slashing and chopping him into small pieces.

"You're putting me on the spot, Jimmy Weak Dog. I can only tell you what I know to be true and tell you truly what has been told to me. Beyond that I cannot say."

"You must see, Arm Long. Must know so then you can say. We must know for true what has happened with our brother."

"I have asked Lieutenant deNunzio to let me see Bird Talks to the Moon, Jimmy Weak Dog. I have explained to him that my badge is not higher than his shoulder boards. Bird Talks committed murder and rape, and he must be punished. Bird Talks is a scout just like you and you and you are scouts. You belong to the army, and it is the army that must punish you if you do wrong or reward you if you do well. My people of the badge have no say in this. I do not ask that Bird Talks be released. I only want to see him so I can tell Pissing Horse and all his brothers that Bird Talks is alive and well. But Lieutenant deNunzio says I cannot see Bird Talks any more than he would allow you to see Bird Talks. I do not know why this is so. I only tell you truly that it is what was told to me."

"Nunzie, his word is no good, Arm Long. Two Face Woman, her word is no good. We must have your word. Or war,

156

Arm Long. We must have truth, or we must have war. Either way, we will do, eh? You tell us which we do."

"I can't tell you what I don't know, Jimmy Weak Dog. I won't lie t' you. I've asked Lieutenant deNunzio to let me see Bird Talks to the Moon. He won't do it. I wish I knew why, but I don't."

"Know why," Swimming Deer said softly from behind Longarm. As a woman she wasn't part of the council circle, but as a proud and independent Ute woman she was right there beside it where she could hear everything that went on.

"What?"

"I know why Lootnant Nunzie won' let nobody see Bird Talks. Lootnant Nunzie, he make promise to Two Face Woman."

"He promised Mrs. Benhurst?"

"To Two Face Woman, yes," Swimming Deer said.

"What does she have to do with it?"

Swimming Deer shrugged. "Last night I serve them. Late late. In Two Face Woman tent. Sojer comes to mess. Old sar'g'nt, he find me there waiting for Long Long to come back. Old sar'g'nt tells me to bring tray to Two Face Woman tent. Lootnant Nunzie is there. Sojer is sent far away. He can't hear nothing. I stay close to take tray back when they are done. I hear what they say. First they eat, you know. Drink a little. Then Two Face Woman suck Lootnant Nunzie. Lootnant Nunzie, he acts like he never does this before. Swears he is in love with Two Face Woman. Two Face Woman, she says she love him, too. Pah. Two Face Woman fucks officer, fucks sojer, too, sometime. Two Face Woman don' love nobody. But she tells Lootnant Nunzie she love him. Wants him to promise to her again that no one ever talk to Bird Talks. She says Bird Talks would brag about fucking her. Then she would be ashamed. That is when she tells Lootnant Nunzie about what Bird Talks do to her when he take her that time. That is when Lootnant Nunzie gets so mad. Lootnant Nunzie, he cuss and he cry and he tells her he will protect her honor, yes? No one will ever be 'lowed to hear Bird Talks brag about fuck-fuck Two Face Woman. That is when he gives her his word. She makes him say it three, four times. He cries and promises and she tells him she loves him. Sucks his pizzle again. Lootnant

157

Nunzie, he is very much in love, yes."

No wonder deNunzio hadn't been willing to bend on the subject, Longarm thought.

But, dammit, deNunzio had to bend. He simply had to.

Longarm sighed. Right. An officer with a code of honor as rigid as Raphael deNunzio's. And Custis Long was supposed to convince him to break his word?

Lots o' luck.

"Is sad," Swimming Deer went on. "So sad."

"What's sad?" Longarm asked.

"Bird Talks, he wouldn' say anything about what he did to Two Face Woman. Even if he could say, he would not. But Two Face Woman and Lootnant Nunzie, they not understand that. Bird Talks could talk in council all night an' never say about fucking Two Face Woman."

"Why is that, Swimming Deer?"

"Because Bird Talks was crazy person when he did what he did, Long Long. If he is right in his head again, he would be too ashame to say what he did."

"Not the murder, surely. I can't believe he would be particularly ashamed of that. You mean he wouldn't want to admit that he raped that woman?"

"Long Long! Really! Bird Talks would say about that. Is only fucking. Everybody does that. No, I know he was crazy person out of head because when he take Two Face Woman and do those things to her, she is bleeding. Now Bird Talks has no power. He touched a woman who was bleeding. Fucked her. How much worse than her shadow falling across him, eh? Now he has no spirit, no power. Now Bird Talks is empty shell."

"That is true, Arm Long," Jimmy Weak Dog put in. "All Ute know Bird Talks to Moon was touched by the spirits. Crazy in head. That is why he must not be beaten. Crazy people must be protected from themselves, Arm Long. Is okay to lock him up. Is good to do this because it protects him. But must not hurt him. That is not allowed."

"Now how in the world would you people know that it was Mrs. Benhurst's time of month? Huh, Swimming Deer? Hell, the woman hadn't even got to the post yet when her husband was murdered. So how would you know about things as personal as her monthly cycle?"

158

Swimming Deer gave him a pitying look, as if to say that she couldn't believe this white man was being so obtuse. "Really, Long Long. Who you think does her laundry when she gets here? Who you think cleans her tent and makes her bed, eh? Ute girl does all that. We always know. Must know. Otherwise, how can we tell Ute man to stay out from shadow of white woman? White woman don't know enough to go to women's lodge when she bleeds. So we watch. We know. We warn Indian man to stay away."

"I'll be damned," Longarm said. "It's logical. I just never thought about it."

"No need, Long Long. Is not the same for you as for Ute."

"Is our way, Arm Long," Jimmy said. "Is why we know Bird Talks is crazy person. We do what we must do, eh? Must do the Ute way. Not white."

"No, I reckon not." Longarm looked around the circle of young warriors.

Tonight they sat together with him. Shared their food with him. Politely refrained from killing him.

Tomorrow these same young men might well be engaged in a life and death struggle. They and all their people.

A handful of Springfield carbines. A few boxes of stolen cartridges. A few sharp knives. They would take those few weapons and declare war on the entire might of the United States Army.

Unless Longarm could think of a way to keep it from happening.

And at the moment, dammit, he couldn't. He . . .

He blinked. And stared.

A handful of Springfield carbines. Some cartridges. Some knives.

Jesus!

Longarm sat bolt upright on the chunk of firewood that was serving him as a chair.

A handful of Springfield carbines.

"Jimmy," he blurted. "I want you t' tell me about being a scout for the U.S. Army. An' about Bird Talks to the Moon, too." He leaned forward now, practically vibrating with the tight-pent excitement of his find. Now, if Jimmy Weak Dog and the other scouts confirmed it . . .

159

Chapter 36

Longarm woke early. He started to get up, then remembered the events of the evening before and dropped his head back onto the pillow.

He smiled and reached for Swimming Deer, who was snuggled warm at his side.

There wasn't any need to get up yet. Not for hours probably.

He didn't have to lie around feeling bored, though. There was plenty he could do to occupy himself for the time being.

Swimming Deer stirred at his touch, and even before she was awake was shifting position to accommodate him. Her body was moist and welcoming to him.

The second time he awakened, considerably later in the forenoon, Longarm yawned and reached for a smoke. Swimming Deer sat up beside him and pulled her dress on. "You are hungry, Long Long?" she asked.

"Kinda."

"Wait here. I will get."

The Ute girl padded outside and was quickly gone. Longarm sat upright, shivered once, and then set about the morning chores of getting ready to face the day.

By the time Swimming Deer returned, he had shit, shaved, and dressed. The girl fetched in a tray of hot food and in her wake dragged in a none too pleased Sergeant Rogers.

"Sir, d'you know what this crazy Injun is up to?" Rogers complained.

"I'm not sure I know what you mean, Sergeant."

"Her and all my other help disappeared last night. There wasn't a one of 'em around to help me with the gentlemen's breakfast this morning, Marshal Long, sir. Do you know what

160

a thing like that does t' my reputation?"

"Sorry, Sergeant. I have to confess that I'm responsible for keeping Swimming Deer away. Wouldn't know 'bout the rest o' your help, though." That wasn't the whole truth, but Rogers didn't need to concern himself with that, Longarm figured.

"If you are quite done with her, sir, I'd like to get along with my lunch preparations now. Swimming Deer?"

The girl looked at Longarm and waited for his nod before she deposited his breakfast tray on the foot of the bed they'd just shared and then consented to go with Rogers back to the officers' mess.

Longarm took his time with breakfast, then stepped outside. It was approaching midday. Ought to be about time, he figured.

"Excuse me, soldier. Could you refresh me 'bout where the headquarters tent is hid?"

The private shrugged and pointed. Longarm thanked the boy politely and then ambled along in the direction the soldier had indicated. He hoped Camp Brunot turned out to be easier to find your way around in once the permanent streets and buildings were in place.

"Sorry, sir, but you can't go in there just now," the duty orderly informed him.

"I understand that you have your orders, son, but I'm afraid an exception's got t' be made in this case. I have t' see the post commander. Right away."

"I repeat, sir. I am sorry, but you cannot see the lieutenant just now. Perhaps if you come back after lunch, sir?"

Longarm smiled. Nodded. Walked around the orderly and through the canvas flap that served First Lieutenant Henry Willis as an office door.

No wonder the orderly had been told to keep visitors away, Longarm saw. The commanding officer of Camp Brunot, Utah, had his head down on his desk and was taking a nap. He was snoring softly, his exhalations fluttering some paperwork on the desk. It really seemed a shame to wake the man.

"Yo! Henry!"

Willis shot upright, a look of consternation spreading over his boyish face. "Wha'?"

"It's okay, Henry. Take your time. Get your wits about you." Longarm turned to the orderly who was yapping at his heels for having come in and disturbed the commander. "You, boy, go fetch Lieutenant deNunzio here. Adjutant's call, son. Right now."

"Sir?"

"You heard me. Jump to it."

"But—"

"Go!" Longarm bawled into the startled young man's face. The soldier spun around and went.

"Is that you, Long? What the hell is this about, man? Why're you barging in here and giving orders to my people?"

"Official business, Henry. As a duly authorized representative of the United States government, Department o' Justice, U.S. Marshal's Office, I am callin' on you and Lieutenant deNunzio t' assist me in the performance o' my duties."

"Pardon me?"

"Far as I know, Willis, you haven't committed no crime and so you don't need no pardon."

The officer blinked. "Lighten up, Henry. I was havin' fun with you there."

"Oh."

"Actually, though, there's no point in going inta all this until we're all together. I'm sure the adjutant will be here in just a minute. What say we wait till then t' go through the formalities. Meantime, whyn't you drag out your book o' regulations an' procedures an' see what all it says about the army . . . which is t' say you . . . givin' aid t' a deputy marshal who's engaged in undertakin' official duties . . . which is t' say me."

"Official duties." Willis scratched the side of his jaw and tried to swallow a yawn.

"Uh-huh."

"You need my assistance."

"Uh-huh."

"I'll look it up."

"You do that, Henry."

"Really, Long. You must tell us more than this vague cock-and-bull story about crimes having been committed and jurisdiction having been determined. You know? We need details, man. Facts."

162

"In a minute, Henry. Just bear with me. I'll make it all clear to you, I promise."

"You'd better," deNunzio snarled. "And quickly."

The three of them—four, actually, Willis's orderly was trotting along behind like an anxious pup sniffing at its master's heels—were walking at a swift pace toward the outskirts of the post.

They broke out of the line of tents, crossed the flat where the freight wagons unloaded stores, and even then Longarm did not turn aside.

"See here, Long, if you think for one moment that we are going to let you visit that Indian because of some trumped-up—"

"No such thing, Raphael. I'm not headed for the guard tent."

"Where then, dammit? The only other thing over here is—"

"That's right," Longarm agreed.

"You are treading thin ice, Long. I'm warning you," deNunzio said.

"I understand. So will you. Just give me a minute."

Henry Willis gasped, and Longarm guessed that the man had finally realized that they weren't exactly alone out here.

Camp Brunot with its people and its activity lay behind. But ahead there were several hundred more people. Ute Indian people.

Pissing Horse, the entire cadre of Ute scouts, virtually every Ute male in the band between the ages of ten and eighty, and very nearly every Ute woman, too, were all lined up on top of a ridge some three hundred yards distant. This was the opportunity Longarm had been waiting for. He had sent word by way of the scouts last night, but it took a while to get an entire village population moved around. And he did want them all to see what happened here today.

"They aren't . . ." First Lieutenant Henry Willis, commanding officer of Camp Brunot and theoretical commander as well of the new Ute Indian reservation, at least until the civilian agency people showed up, sounded downright nervous at the sight of all those Indians in front of him.

"No, Henry, they ain't fixing to run down an' slaughter you. Not t'day anyhow. If it makes you feel any better, Pissing

Horse gave me his word that t'day all he'll do is watch an' see what happens. If he decides he wants t' fight you, Henry, he'll wait till tomorrow."

Lieutenant Willis tugged at his coattails and tried to look unconcerned.

"An Indian's word?" deNunzio asked.

"I'd accept your word, Raphael, an' I don't know you half as good as I know Pissing Horse. There's lots o' things that old Indian would lie about. This ain't one of 'em. He's given me until tomorrow t' get things square. There won't be no massacre—at least until then."

"There is that small favor, I suppose. But I still do not understand what possible reason you could have for—"

"Patience, Raphael. We're almost there now."

Lieutenant deNunzio grumped and grunted and marched onward. Lieutenant Willis squirmed and twitched and kept sending nervous glances toward the ridgetop where the Ute were standing.

"Do they have to stare like that?"

"Watching is what they come here t' do, Henry. Looking at us beats shooting at us, though, don't it?"

"Marginally," Willis agreed. He didn't sound happy about it.

The sentry posted outside Mrs. Clytemnestra Benhurst's tent snapped sharply to attention and slapped the stock of his rifle to present arms. He didn't bother hollering for anyone to halt, presumably because the entire complement of Camp Brunot's commissioned officers was with the party bearing down on him.

"Shall I announce callers, sir?"

Willis turned to Longarm and raised an eyebrow.

"Yeah, Abner, you go ahead an' do that."

"Very good, sir." Abner grounded his rifle, wheeled, and went to tap on the front tent pole. He said something too low for the gentlemen to overhear, then wheeled back around and scurried to his post. "The lady will need a few minutes before she receives visitors, sirs."

"Thank you, Abner."

"Yes, sir."

"Cigar anybody?" There were no takers. Longarm lighted one for himself and stood perfectly relaxed while he smoked it. Willis and deNunzio both looked on edge, but neither said anything.

The few minutes turned to ten and ten to twenty, but eventually Mrs. Benhurst made her appearance. Her hair looked freshly fixed, and her shirtwaist was crisp and spotless. She gave the gentlemen a nod and graced them with a smile. "You wished to see me, Lieutenant Willis?"

"It is, um, actually Marshal Long here who wants to see you, ma'am. He asked Lieutenant deNunzio and myself to accompany him. Something to do with army cooperation into an official investigation undertaken by the, um, Justice Department. I assured him that we would all cooperate to the fullest extent possible. Speaking for the personnel of the regiment, that is. Naturally, madam, you are not bound by this."

"But, naturally, sir, I shall be glad to cooperate with the marshal in any way that I can. My late husband would have expected no less of me, I am sure." She smiled.

"Very well, Marshal. You may proceed."

Longarm nodded. He paced a bit as he talked. He doubted that either officer noticed that the pacing placed Longarm in a position from which he could fire at either of the officers or at the enlisted men if the need for that should arise. Not that he expected it to. Exactly.

"If I can explain a few points about a deputy marshal's jurisdiction," Longarm said, "a marshal has the responsibility t' act whenever there's a federal crime committed, and he becomes aware of it. Or whenever there's a federal warrant issued or under certain other circumstances. What we're looking at here is the commission of a crime that falls under the federal statutes an' therefore under my jurisdiction. Follow me so far?"

"Please get on with it, Long," deNunzio growled. "The lady has better things to do than listen to you."

"Of course she does. Sorry." He smiled but didn't sound or look the least bit sorry. "Anyway, gentlemen, when an employee of the U.S. government is murdered, the crime automatic like comes under federal jurisdiction. Unless both the murderer and the victim are military personnel, in which case the branch o' service involved takes care o' the prosecution itself."

"Long, if you are getting at this Bird Talks business—"

"As a matter o' fact, Lieutenant, I am not. Not actually. No, what I'm looking at is the murder o' three government employees by a civilian who is not either a soldier nor an enrolled employee o' the army. Which I think you would agree rules out the Ute scout Bird Talks to the Moon."

"Well, I'm glad to hear that, Long. Carry on, please."

"Thank you, gentlemen. Mrs. Clytemnestra Benhurst, I am placing you under arrest for the murder of Major Donald Benhurst and two army enlisted personnel, whose names I'll hafta get later when we make out the paperwork."

"What!" DeNunzio's roar was loud enough that it probably could be heard by the Ute who were watching in the distance. "Are you out of your mind, man? Private! Ready your musket. If this man makes any move toward the lady, you are to shoot. Is that clear, Private? You are to shoot."

The private didn't answer. Didn't look all that ready to shoot, either. But he did go as far as to lift his rifle and hold it at waist level in a sort of shocked approximation of port arms.

"You want me t' explain how I know she's the one murdered those men, Raphael?" Longarm asked.

"Explain, hell. What I demand, sir, is a retraction. You will retract, by God, or I'll see you on the field of honor, sir."

"Quit playin' tin soldier, Raphael, an' listen t' reason for a change. First off, the lady don't love you any more'n she loves Abner. Who she also screws whenever he's the only one handy. Don't she, Abner?" Longarm shook his head. "Naw, don't say it out loud, son. We can see from the red on your cheeks what the answer is."

"You sonofabitch," Sly said.

"From you, Sly, I'd be upset t' be called anything else. Raphael, that woman there has been blowing smoke out her shapely ass since before she ever got here. You want me t' prove it? I can, you know. I got to, in fact, or the jury won't never convict her. But to prove what I got in mind, Raphael, all anyone has t' do is pay attention t' the facts. All of 'em, though, an' not just the few Miz Benhurst wants remembered.

"One fact that has got lost in the midst of everything else is that three men, three army men, were all o' them shot down while they was taking a leak. Three men, mind, who know something about guns an' courage an' doing the things that got to be done. Yet there they were, all of them shot down together at one an' the same time. Now, what I want t' ask you is this, Raphael. What kinda arms d' your scouts—like Bird Talks to the Moon—what kinda arms d' they carry?"

The adjutant frowned. A moment later Willis did, too.

"That's right, boys. Bird Talks to the Moon was armed only with a single-shot Springfield carbine an' a knife. He didn't own a revolver. There aren't any issued to the scouts, and he didn't have one o' his own. Nobody in Pissing Horse's band is rich enough to have a toy like that. Which a pistol is to an Indian. Which means that either Bird Talks to the Moon is one hellacious hand with a trapdoor carbine . . . or he wasn't the one that all alone shot those boys down that day.

"Now, I'll give you something else t' chew on. The girls that clean Miz Benhurst's tent say she's got some silky, lacy, nice-smelling stuff tucked in the top tray o' her travel trunk. Those girls know 'cause they've took it all out an' held it up to themselves an' admired the pretties. But y' know what else is in that tray, buried underneath the unmentionables? A big ol' revolver. A LeMat, judging from what they describe to me. You know the LeMat, deNunzio? O' course you do. Big ol' clunky thing, but it fires eight pistol balls from the cylinder an' one shotgun shell from the center barrel. Plenty of firepower in a LeMat, boys. Enough, say, to murder three surprised men, even army men, before they could do anything about it.

"And something else you never knew 'cause nobody ever questioned the lady's story enough to ask. Miz Benhurst was on the rag that day. Which don't mean much to you and me, but to a Indian like Bird Talks, it woulda meant she was purely taboo no matter how worked up an' horny he mighta been. Even if all the rest of it had been true, boys, he wouldn't 've touched that woman. By his lights he couldn't 've screwed that white woman without cursing himself an' throwing away his manhood. An' that'd be an awful price to pay.

"No, the way I see it, boys, now that I've started looking at more than just a select few facts, Miz Benhurst herself is the one that did the killing that day. Bird Talks likely came along afterward an' was trying to rescue her, not kidnap her. Then

167

when your soldier boys showed up, she hollered rape nice an' quick. Prob'ly really worried her that Bird Talks wasn't shot down on the spot. That's what she was hoping for at the time, I'd bet. But she covered over and made the best of things right well since then, wouldn't you say?" Longarm smiled benignly at the widow Benhurst.

"You can't be right, Long. Can't possibly be."

"Raphael, you don't sound like you believe that your own self. But I tell you what. Just to get an eyewitness view from somebody that ain't ever been asked for his side o' the story, why don't we all of us sashay over an' see what Bird Talks to the Moon has t' say? Let's just see how close his story is to mine. Which I might point out he hasn't never had a chance to hear. Or how close it is t' Miz Benhurst's tale o' rape an' murder an' assorted treachery."

"Darling—your promise. Don't forget your promise," Sly Benhurst yelped.

"It's a bad thing, Raphael, when a man is caught between his spoken promise and his sworn duties," Longarm said.

DeNunzio looked sick.

"You might keep in mind that a promise wrongfully gained ain't the same as one honestly gotten."

"Orderly. Go fetch the prisoner Bird Talks."

"Yes, sir." The headquarters orderly came to attention, saluted, and went quick-timing off in the direction of the guard tent.

"I can't believe any of this," Willis mumbled.

"Of course you can't, Henry," Sly Benhurst purred. "The marshal there is jealous, that's all. He tried to force himself on me, you know. I rebuffed him, and he swore he would get even. This is just his sick attempt to strike back at me for refusing him."

"For God's sake, Cly. Don't." It was deNunzio who made that appeal. Love might be blind, but it wasn't always utterly stupid as well.

"You shall see. You all shall. Just wait until that savage gets here. He'll tell you himself what he did to me. He will brag on it. And I shall be humiliated. The honor of this entire regiment will be besmirched. Oh, they will hear about this back at regimental headquarters. I am known there, you know.

168

Favorably known. I've always been a favorite of the gentlemen there. It was only my stupid husband who wanted this posting. Can you believe it? He actually wanted to come here? But Donald is dead now, isn't he? And I still have my admirers at headquarters. They know me there. They will respond when they hear how you have treated me today. And on your heads will it be, gentlemen. On your heads. Now, if you will excuse me, I shall retire to my quarters. Call me when the savage is here. I demand the right to face him."

Willis came to attention and bobbed his head as the woman—not a lady, though—sniffed loudly and disappeared inside her tent. DeNunzio didn't even do that much. He just looked away.

Longarm sighed and reached for another cheroot. He was thinking that Sly Benhurst had as good as told them the reason for her crimes. The silly cunt. She was upset to be taken away from the comforts of civilized surroundings and dragged out here in the middle of nowhere. It was a problem she'd chosen to solve in a rather extreme manner. Longarm had been wondering why she'd done it. Now he suspected he knew. He hoped it wouldn't be long until they brought Bird Talks over. He wanted this done with.

In fact, it was close to a half hour later before a puzzled guard detachment arrived with Bird Talks supported between them. The Ute scout had to be virtually carried after the beating deNunzio had given him. But there was no question that the man was alive.

It did no harm, Longarm realized, that the Ute could see as much for themselves now.

He looked up toward the ridge, but for some reason the damned Indians were paying no attention to their own kinsman at the moment. Instead, they were all gathered in a small, silent knot at the near end of the ridgeline.

If Longarm hadn't known better, he would have thought they might all be lumped into a prayer session. Except this band was far from being Christianized. Besides, for some reason the men were grouped on the outside of the tight circle, which meant that the women were inside it. Longarm couldn't recall ever seeing any ceremony that would call for something like that.

Damned odd, he thought. Oh, well.

"Abner, I think you can call the lady out now if you please."

"Yes, sir." The soldier went forward and tapped lightly on the tent pole. Then tapped again. "Ma'am? Mrs. Benhurst, ma'am? Sly?" He cleared his throat.

"Go inside, soldier," deNunzio ordered. "Present the commanding officer's compliments and inform the lady that her presence is required."

"Shouldn't that be requested, sir?"

" 'Required' is what I said, soldier. 'Required' is what I intended."

"Yes, sir." Abner slipped inside the tent. A moment later he came back out. "Sir? The lady, sir. She ain't there. And there's a big cut in the back wall. I think she run out, sir. I think she's got away."

"Damn," Willis said.

"We'll find her," deNunzio swore.

Longarm shook his head and reached for another cheroot. Unless he missed his guess, there wasn't any need for the army to go looking for Mrs. Clytemnestra Benhurst.

She was, he suspected, up atop that ridge yonder.

Or what was left of her would be up there, anyhow.

Longarm frankly wasn't sure if he should feel bad about that or not. He didn't feel bad about it. Though maybe he ought to.

"I, uh, reckon I'll walk up an' have a word with Pissing Horse," he said. "Be all right if I take Bird Talks with me? I think his folks 'd like to have him back now."

The army personnel barely acknowledged the request. But then they were busy rushing about trying to organize a search party for Mrs. Benhurst.

Longarm took Lieutenant Willis's grunt for consent and began helping Bird Talks to the Moon up the slope toward his people. He didn't have to help the young scout very far. As soon as the Ute noticed what was happening, they came streaming down to help. The men did, anyway. The women were still busy up on top of the ridge. Longarm took a look in that direction and shuddered. Then looked away.

"You're all right now, son," he said as eager hands reached out to take Bird Talks to the Moon from him.

Watch for

LONGARM IN THE SIERRA ORIENTAL

159th in the bold LONGARM series
from Jove

Coming in March!

NELSON NYE

The Baron of Blood & Thunder

Two-time winner of the Western Writers of America's Golden Spur Award and winner of the Levi Strauss Golden Saddleman Award . . . with over 50,000,000 copies of his books in print.

NELSON NYE

Author of RIDER ON THE ROAN, TROUBLE AT QUINN'S CROSSING, THE SEVEN SIX-GUNNERS, THE PARSON OF GUNBARREL BASIN, LONG RUN, GRINGO, THE LOST PADRE, TREASURE TRAIL FROM TUCSON, and dozens of others, is back with his most exciting Western adventure yet. . . .

THE LAST CHANCE KID

Born to English nobility, Alfred Addlington wants nothing more than to become an American cowboy. With his family's reluctant permission, Alfred becomes just that . . . and gets much more than he bargained for when he gets mixed up with horse thieves, crooked ranchers, and a band of prairie rats who implicate him in one crime after another!

Turn the page
for an exciting preview of
THE LAST CHANCE KID
by Nelson Nye!

My name is Alfred Addlington. Some may find it hard to believe I was born in New York City. I never knew my mother. Father is a lord; I suppose you would call him a belted earl. The family never cared for Mother. Marrying a commoner if you are of the nobility is far worse, it was felt, than murdering someone.

I was, of course, educated in England. As a child I'd been an avid reader, and always at the back of my mind was this horrible obsession to one day become a Wild West cowboy. I'd no need to run away—transportation was happily furnished. While I was in my seventeenth year my youthful peccadillos were such that I was put on a boat bound for America, made an allowance and told never to come back.

They've been hammering outside. I have been in this place now more than four months and would never have believed it could happen to me, but the bars on my window are truly there, and beyond the window they are building a gallows. So I'd better make haste if I'm to get this all down.

I do not lay my being here to a "broken home" or evil companions. I like to feel in some part it is only a matter of justice miscarried, though I suppose most any rogue faced with the rope is bound to consider himself badly used. But you shall judge for yourself.

Seventeen I was when put aboard that boat, and I had a wealth of experience before at nineteen this bad thing caught up with me.

So here I was again in America. In a number of ways it was a peculiar homecoming. First thing I did after clearing customs was get aboard a train that would take me into those great open spaces I'd so long been entranced with. It brought me to New Mexico and a town called Albuquerque, really an overgrown village from which I could see the Watermellon Mountains.

I found the land and the sky and the brilliant sunshine remarkably stimulating. Unlike in the British Midlands the air was clean and crisply invigorating. But no one would have me. At the third ranch I tried they said, "Too young. We got no time to break in a raw kid with roundup scarce two weeks away."

At that time I'd no idea of the many intricacies or the harsh realities of the cow business. You might say I had on a pair of rose-colored glasses. I gathered there might be quite a ruckus building up in Lincoln County, a sort of large-scale feud from all I could learn, so I bought myself a horse, a pistol and a J. B. Stetson hat and headed for the action.

In the interests of saving time and space I'll only touch on the highlights of these preliminaries, recording full details where events became of impelling importance.

Passing through Seven Oaks, I met Billy, a chap whose name was on everyone's tongue, though I could not think him worth half the talk. To me he seemed hard, mean spirited and stupid besides. He made fun of my horse, calling it a crowbait, declared no real gent would be found dead even near it. Turned out he knew of a first class mount he'd be glad to secure for me if I'd put one hundred dollars into his grubby hand. He was a swaggering sort I was glad to be rid of. Feeling that when in Rome one did as the Romans, I gave him the hundred dollars, not expecting ever to see him again, but hoping in these strange surroundings I would not be taken for a gullible "greenhorn."

A few days later another chap, who said his name was Jesse Evans, advised me to steer clear of Billy. "A bad lot," he told me. "A conniving double-crosser." When I mentioned giving Billy the hundred dollars on the understanding he would provide a top horse, he said with a snort and kind of pitying look, "You better bid that money good-bye right now."

But three days later, true to his word, Billy rode up to the place I was lodging with a fine horse in tow. During my schooling back in England I had learned quite a bit about horses, mostly hunters and hacks and jumpers and a few that ran in "flat" races for purses, and this mount Billy fetched looked as good as the best. "Here, get on him," Billy urged. "See what you think, and if he won't do I'll find you another."

"He'll do just fine," I said, taking the lead shank, "and here's ten dollars for your kindness."

With that lopsided grin he took the ten and rode off.

I rode the new horse over to the livery and dressed him in my saddle and bridle while the proprietor eyed me with open mouth. "Don't tell me that's yours," he finally managed, still looking as if he couldn't believe what he saw.

"He surely is. Yes, indeed. Gave a hundred dollars for him."

Just as I was about to mount up, a mustached man came bustling into the place. "Stop right there!" this one said across the glint of a pistol. "I want to know what you're doing with the Major's horse. Speak up or it'll be the worse for you."

"What Major?"

"Major Murphy. A big man around here."

"Never heard of him. I bought this horse for one hundred dollars."

"Bought it, eh? Got a bill of sale?"

"Well, no," I said. "Didn't think to ask for one."

I'd discovered by this time the man with the gun had a star on his vest. His expression was on the skeptical side. He wheeled on the liveryman. "You sell him that horse?"

"Not me! Came walkin' in here with it not ten minutes ago."

"I'm goin' to have to hold you, young feller," the man with the star said, pistol still aimed at my belt buckle. "A horse thief's the lowest scoundrel I know of."

A shadow darkened the doorway just then and Jesse Evans stepped in. "Hang on a bit, Marshal. I'll vouch for this button. If he told you he paid for this horse it's the truth. Paid it to Billy—I'll take my oath on it."

A rather curious change reshaped the marshal's features. "You sure of that, Evans?"

"Wouldn't say so if I wasn't."

The marshal looked considerably put out. "All right," he said to me, "looks like you're cleared. But I'm confiscatin'

177

this yere horse; I'll see it gits back to the rightful owner. You're free to go, but don't let me find you round here come sundown." And he went off with the horse.

"Never mind," Evans said. "Just charge it up to experience. But was I you I'd take the marshal's advice and hunt me another habitation." And he grinned at me sadly. "I mean pronto— right now."

Still rummaging my face, he said, scrubbing a fist across his own, "Tell you what I'll do," and led me away out of the livery-keeper's hearing. "I've got a reasonably good horse I'll let you have for fifty bucks. Even throw in a saddle—not so handsome as the one you had but durable and sturdy. You interested?"

Once stung, twice shy. "Let's see him," I said, and followed him out to a corral at the far edge of town. I looked the horse over for hidden defects but could find nothing wrong with it; certainly the animal should be worth fifty dollars. Firmly I said, "I'll be wanting a bill of sale."

"Of course," he chuckled. "Naturally." Fetching a little blue notebook out of a pocket, he asked politely, "What name do you go by?"

"My own," I said. "Alfred Addlington."

He wrote it down with a flourish. "All right, Alfie." He tore the page from his book and I put it in my wallet while Jesse saddled and bridled my new possession. I handed him the money, accepted the reins and stepped into the saddle.

He said, "I'll give you a piece of advice you can take or cock a snook at. Notice you're packin' a pistol. Never put a hand anyplace near it without you're aimin' to use it. Better still," he said, looking me over more sharply, "get yourself a shotgun, one with two barrels. Nobody'll laugh at that kind of authority."

"Well, thanks. Where do I purchase one?"

"Be a-plenty at Lincoln if that's where you're headed. Any gun shop'll have 'em."

I thanked him again and, having gotten precise directions, struck out for the county seat feeling I'd been lucky to run across such a good Samaritan. I was a pretty fair shot with handgun or rifle but had discovered after much practice I could be killed and buried before getting my pistol into speaking position. So Evans's advice about acquiring a shotgun seemed additional evidence of the good will he bore me.

It was shortly after noon the next day when I came up the dirt road into Lincoln. For all practical purposes it was a one-street town, perhaps half a mile long, flanked by business establishments, chief amongst them being the two-storey Murphy-Dolan store building. I recall wondering if this was the Major whose stolen horse Billy'd sold me, later discovering it was indeed. Leaving my horse at a hitch rack I went inside to make inquiries about finding a job.

The gentleman I talked with had an Irish face underneath a gray derby. After listening politely he informed me he was Jimmie Dolan—the Dolan of the establishment—and could offer me work as a sort of handyman if such wasn't beneath my dignity. If I showed aptitude, he said, there'd be a better job later and he would start me off at fifty cents a day.

I told him I'd take it.

"If you've a horse there's a carriage shed back of the store where you can leave him and we'll sell you oats at a discount," he added.

"I'd been hoping to get on with some ranch," I said.

"A fool's job," said Dolan with a grimace. "Long hours, hard work, poor pay and no future," he assured me. "You string your bets with us and you'll get to be somebody while them yahoos on ranches are still punchin' cows."

I went out to feed, water and put up my new horse. There was a man outside giving it some pretty hard looks. "This your nag?" he asked as I came up.

"It most certainly is."

"Where'd you get it?"

"Bought it in Seven Oaks a couple of days ago. Why?"

He eyed me some more. "Let's see your bill of sale, bub," and brushed back his coat to display a sheriff's badge pinned to his shirt.

I dug out the paper I had got from Evans. The sheriff studied it and then, much more searching, studied me. "Expect you must be new around here if you'd take Evans's word for anything. I'm taking it for granted you bought the horse in good faith, but I'm going to have to relieve you of it. This animal's the property of a man named Tunstall, stolen from him along with several others about a week ago."

I was pretty riled up. "This," I said angrily, "is the second stolen mount I've been relieved of in the past ten days. Don't you have any honest men in your bailiwick?"

"A few, son. Not many I'll grant you. You're talkin' to one now as it happens."

"Then where can I come by a horse that's not stolen?"

That blue stare rummaged my face again. "You a limey?"

"If you mean do I hail from England, yes. I came here hoping to get to be a cowboy, but nobody'll have me."

He nodded. "It's a hard life, son, an' considerably underpaid. Takes time to learn, but you seem young enough to have plenty of that. How much did you give for the two stolen horses?"

"One hundred and fifty dollars."

He considered me again. "You're pretty green, I guess. Most horses in these parts sell for forty dollars."

"A regular Johnny Raw," I said bitterly.

"Well . . . a mite gullible," the sheriff admitted. "Reckon time will cure that if you live long enough. Being caught with a stolen horse hereabouts is a hangin' offense. Come along," he said. "I'll get you a horse there's no question about, along with a bona fide set of papers to prove it. Do you have forty dollars?"

I told him I had and, counting out the required sum, handed it to him. He picked up the reins of Tunstall's horse, and we walked down the road to a public livery and feed corral. The sheriff told the man there what we wanted and the fellow fetched out a good-looking sorrel mare.

"This here's a mite better'n average, Sheriff—oughta fetch eighty. Trouble is these fool cowhands won't ride anythin' but geldin's. I guarantee this mare's a real goer. Try her out, boy. If you're satisfied, she's yours fer forty bucks."

The sheriff, meanwhile, had got my gear off Tunstall's horse. "Get me a lead shank," he said to the stableman. Transferring my saddle and bridle to the mare I swung onto her, did a few figure eights, put her into a lope, walked her around and proclaimed myself satisfied. The animal's name it seemed was Singlefoot. "She'll go all day at that rockin' chair gait," the man said. "Comfortable as two six-shooters in the same belt."

Thanking them both, I rode her over to the nearest café, tied her securely to the hitch pole in front of it and went in to put some food under my belt, pleased to see she looked very well alongside the tail-switchers already tied there.

If you enjoyed this book, subscribe now and get...

TWO FREE

A $7.00 VALUE–

If you would like to read more of the very best, most exciting, adventurous, action-packed Westerns being published today, you'll want to subscribe to True Value's Western Home Subscription Service.

Each month the editors of True Value will select the 6 very best Westerns from America's leading publishers for special readers like you. You'll be able to preview these new titles as soon as they are published, *FREE* for ten days with no obligation!

TWO FREE BOOKS

When you subscribe, we'll send you your first month's shipment of the newest and best 6 Westerns for you to preview. With your first shipment, two of these books will be yours as our introductory gift to you absolutely *FREE* (a $7.00 value), regardless of what you decide to do. If

you like them, as much as we think you will, keep all six books but pay for just 4 at the low subscriber rate of just $2.75 each. If you decide to return them, keep 2 of the titles as our gift. No obligation.

Special Subscriber Savings

When you become a True Value subscriber you'll save money several ways. First, all regular monthly selections will be billed at the low subscriber price of just $2.75 each. That's at least a savings of $4.50 each month below the publishers price. Second, there is never any shipping, handling or other hidden charges—*Free home delivery*. What's more there is no minimum number of books you must buy, you may return any selection for full credit and you can cancel your subscription at any time. A TRUE VALUE!